RIDE BY NIGHT

OTHER BOOKS IN THE PONY LIBRARY INCLUDE

WISH FOR A PONY
CARGO OF HORSES
NO ENTRY
STOLEN PONIES
WE HUNTED HOUNDS
RIDERS FROM AFAR
HORSES AT HOME
I WANTED A PONY
RIDING WITH THE LYNTONS
PONY CLUB CAMP
PONY CLUB TEAM
ONE DAY EVENT
STABLE TO LET
FIRST PONY
JACKY JUMPS TO THE TOP
PONIES ON THE HEATHER
THE SURPRISE RIDING CLUB
A PONY FOR TWO
CLEAR ROUND
AFRAID TO RIDE
REBEL PONY
THE TRICK JUMPERS
A PONY FOR SALE
WE RODE TO THE SEA
THREE PONIES AND SHANNAN
I HAD TWO PONIES
SHOW JUMPING SECRET
BLACK HUNTING WHIP
PONY SURPRISE

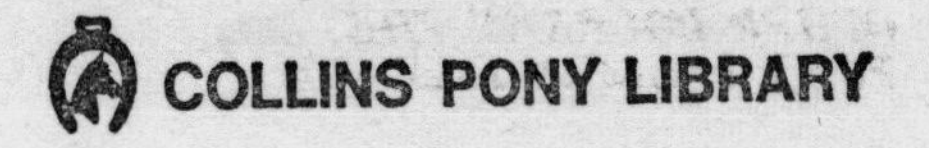

RIDE BY NIGHT

Christine Pullein-Thompson

Text Illustrations by
Sheila Rose

COLLINS
LONDON & GLASGOW

First printed in this new edition 1974

ISBN 0 00 164325 8

PRINTED AND MADE IN GREAT BRITAIN BY
WILLIAM COLLINS SONS AND CO. LTD.
LONDON AND GLASGOW

CHAPTER ONE

IT was Desmond who first suggested a camping holiday. We were on a small hill watching the perimeter, while our Western Island ponies, Skylark and Sandpiper, cropped the grass. A plane landed. In the distance behind us, mountains raised majestic peaks to a summer sky.

"Camping? And where would we go?" I asked stupidly. I was chewing a blade of hill grass. Black-faced sheep watched us; a curlew drifted in the sky. It was a lazy kind of day, a day to dream impossible dreams. I didn't think my brother was serious.

"Here of course. Other children camp in the summer holidays. It's not our fault the Pony Club's so small. We can get up a party."

His voice told me that he was serious. He was looking intently at the Air Force Base, but his eyes weren't seeing it—he was seeing a row of tents, sleeping-bags, camping equipment.

"We'll take the ponies; perhaps an extra pack pony. It'll be super. We'll stop by burns and buy provisions as we go. We won't plan much. We'll look for adventure," said my brother.

"What about Mummy and Daddy?"

"The age limit will be sixteen. We'll average twenty miles a day. Think of it, Sheila!" cried Desmond.

He began to laugh, looking more like a small boy than someone rising fifteen. His eyes had that look which I knew too well, the look which had got us into trouble so often in the past—"Sheila, let's ride tonight by moonlight"—"Sheila, let's see how far we can walk"—"Sheila, let's paint the nursery chairs green"—and had brought home school reports which called him "wild," "irresponsible," someone "whose high spirits defeat his common sense."

"It's just one of your wild ideas. Mummy and Daddy will never agree," I said, standing up.

"Defeatist. But you'll see—a week from now we'll be camping," cried Desmond.

"But who with?" I asked.

"There'll be two tents, one for girls and one for boys. There will be Leslie."

"Leslie! But she'll never camp. She's got a nanny. She's rich," I objected. "Anyway we hardly know her. We hardly know anyone if it comes to that . . ."

"And Roderick, or Roddy or whatever you like to call him. And Jennifer and John, Bruce and Hamish, Susan Picton," continued Desmond obstinately.

"You're suggesting the whole Pony Club. And Jennifer and Susan are sure to cry," I complained. "And probably nothing will happen. And they'll hate it. They like organised games and an instructor standing in the middle."

"And we'll all take dogs . . ."

I could see the tour now: the cavalcade of riders with ropes slung round their ponies' necks, the mixture of dogs following. The tents dotted across a valley. For a week there would be no real washing up. No: "Sheila, tidy your room."

"But supposing no one wants to come?" I asked.

"They'll come. There's nothing happening at all the week after next. No rallies, no shows."

"We'll need mackintoshes," I said.

"If we have room to carry them. We have to think of the ponies," replied Desmond.

"And there will be no rules. Everyone will do as they like."

"Exactly. You've got the idea," cried Desmond.

So the idea was born and we rode down to the little village called Collaig with our heads in the clouds.

"We'll have to ask Mummy and Daddy tonight," said Desmond as we untacked the ponies in the yard behind the cottage where we live.

The perimeter was quiet now. Men stood about near the hangars chatting. In the still green sea there was a variety of boats; and a few tiny children were playing on the clean white sand in the bay.

We turned the ponies into the rough paddock alongside the cottage and they rolled over and over; and now the sun was low above the hills.

"You see we must do something. Time is passing. This is our third summer here. And what have we done? Nothing," cried my brother contemptuously.

"What do other people do?" I asked.

"Camp!" cried Desmond.

We went indoors. Our retriever rose to welcome us. The kitchen was tidy and quiet.

"We'll have to buy tin mugs, and you'll need a pocket knife; better get one with a hoof pick. We'll carry a few oats . . . It'll need a lot of planning," Desmond said. "I'd better find a piece of paper."

"We haven't asked Mummy and Daddy yet," I reminded him.

"They don't seem to be in. Let's get everything fixed first," said Desmond, finding a pencil.

We wrote down a list of names and ponies beside them. Then we started to discuss tents. I was for buying ex-Army ones; Desmond favoured writing to London for them.

"Then there's the beds," I said.

"Sleeping-bags, you mean," cried Desmond. "We can't carry beds."

"Isn't it all going to come to a great deal of money?"

"Everyone who goes must suscribe. We'll form a kind of company—Horse and Dog Campers Limited."

"The Happy Wanderers sounds nicer," I answered. I was becoming elated too, caught in the tide of Desmond's enthusiasm.

"Anyway I've got fifteen pounds in the post office," said Desmond.

Our parents came in then and Desmond said: "It's now or never. Pray," and we went into the sitting-room. "Can we go camping?" asked Desmond.

"Wait until I get my slippers on," answered Daddy. "And get the dog off my chair." (Our retriever, Miracle, always seems to be on Daddy's chair when he wants it.) "And someone switch on the news," he continued.

"Has anyone put the kettle on?" asked Mummy, who is tall and slim and Irish with my blue eyes, but with Desmond's gay, wild look about her. Desmond and Daddy share the same determined chin, the same brown eyes; but whereas Daddy's hair is black, Desmond's is a tawny brown which changes in different lights and climates, from chestnut to brown. He is broader than I am, and though we're twins, we're not identical and not alike.

I hurried to the kitchen and lit the Calor gas and filled the kettle. I could hear the six o'clock news, but though the words came to me clearly, they didn't register; I thought, they must say yes. How can anyone object? There's safety in numbers. Parents want their children to be independent and adventurous. I hope Leslie refuses. I can't see her in a tent . . . Jennifer, John and Hamish may be all right; Roderick will be . . .

Mummy came into the kitchen followed by Desmond.

"You must ask your father. It needs thinking about. Supposing you set your tent alight . . ." Mummy said.

"But we won't. We're fourteen. We're not little kids any more," argued Desmond.

"We'll discuss it over tea. Will you lay the table? It's getting late," Mummy said.

We laid the table. There were scones, a cake I had made the day before; digestive biscuits. It was a tea which we were never to forget, because in a sense it was the beginning of everything . . .

"Now what's this about camping?" asked Daddy, taking a scone.

Desmond started to explain. I couldn't look at him; I was too afraid the answer would be "No."

There was a silence when Desmond stopped talking. I thought, it's going to be "No."

"There's safety in numbers, isn't there? And we could ring you up every day," I said.

Mummy and Daddy were looking at one another. Miracle put her head on my knee. It seemed the longest moment of my life.

"We had better see what the other parents say," said my father at last.

It wasn't yes, but neither was it no; there was still hope, and many castles can be built on hope.

Desmond reeled off a lot of names.

"We're all going to take dogs," I said.

"Supposing they fight?" asked Mummy.

"They know one another," I answered.

"We'll be taking first aid kit," said Desmond, determined to sound competent.

Once tea was over the telephoning started.

Desmond rang Leslie first. I stood at his elbow ready to add my voice to his.

"It sounds a whish idea," she said. "I could bring Ching Poo and Rascal, and two ponies if you want two—Ringleader and Raspberry. I think Silver's too small unless you know anyone who would like to borrow him. I've got a tent as well . . ." It's something to be rich, I thought. Three ponies, a tent two dogs . . .

"I don't think Ching Poo. He'll never keep up," my brother said.

"But you've no idea how sporting Pekes are!" cried Leslie. "Honestly, he can keep up with any horse."

They started to argue about Ching Poo. I went back to the kitchen to help with the washing-up.

"Well?" asked Mummy.

"I think Leslie's coming."

"Has she asked her parents?"

"Not yet, but people say she can twist them round her little finger."

"What about Nanny?" asked Mummy.

"Perhaps she can be bribed," I suggested.

We rang everyone we knew with ponies. By the time we had finished our hands were stiff from holding the receiver and bed-time had come. Outside there was a mist, but we could still see the runways dark and shiny from our bedroom windows. The hangars looked queer and a little ghostly in the evening light. They didn't seem to belong; it was as though the hills said, you're here for the moment, but we're here for ever. They were unacceptable aliens, and in the dusk the hills seemed to be frowning.

We stood in my small bedroom and could hear the ponies cropping the grass, and Desmond said, "Let's tick the yesses."

He brought out the list of names and we switched on the light and Desmond said, "Leslie yes. Roddy yes. Jennifer and John probably yes, Hamish no, Susan uncertain. How many does that make?"

"Six counting us," I answered.

"And Bruce Macdonald was out," said Desmond.

"What about the dogs?" I asked.

"Miracle, Rascal, not Ching Poo—I put my foot down—Roddy's West Highland, Cockade, and John's Alsatian, Fearless."

"It's an awful mixture," I said.

"Well, the ponies are just as bad."

"What about parents? Roddy's were all right."

"The others will ring if they say no. But I kept stressing that it would all be properly organised. That we could be visited at any time, that we'd ring up every day. I think everyone's just as bored as we are sometimes. I mean, it would be different if there were gymkhanas and things in the hols."

I couldn't agree with him there. For me the "wine-red moors" and the ponies were enough. I couldn't see enough of them, and because of that I quite suddenly wanted to camp more than anything else in the world.

So we sat chewing pencils and making plans, having no idea how much was to happen to us on our wild adventure. Outside there was the screech of gulls, the soft sound of a peaceful sea.

We heard a plane coming into land before we parted. I washed and climbed into bed. I could smell the heather and the broom outside. I remembered Manchester, Plymouth; the smell of the streets; the lamp-light, the gas-works, the ceaseless roar of traffic. The future seemed unbelievably lovely. We seemed to have everything, as I lay there—a pony each, a dog, wonderful parents. I thought, there will be peace among the hills, no rushing anywhere. I hope we like our companions. I remembered them as I had seen them last, attending a lecture on Stable Management given by Captain Neil Munro, M.R.C.V.S. Jennifer and John had stayed together. Leslie had been elegantly attired in slacks and a hacking jacket, but then anything she wore immediately became elegant, I decided. She had asked intelligent questions. Roddy had won top marks for the quiz. There weren't many other people. I had disgraced myself by falling over a wheel-barrow.

Mummy interrupted my remembering.

"You haven't had a bath. You'll have to have one tomorrow," she said, kissing me. "Don't have camping nightmares."

"Do you think we can go?"

"I think so, but there will have to be certain conditions," Mummy answered, sitting on my bed. "You'll have to be sensible. Sometimes you're not very."

"I know," I agreed sadly.

"We may have to put someone older in charge."

"Oh, no. There isn't anyone," I cried.

"That's the trouble," agreed Mummy, tiptoeing from my room.

CHAPTER TWO

No one subscribed, but we managed to collect three tents and everyone promised to provide a sleeping-bag and two saddle-bags. And then all the parents got together and everything was ruined; or so it seemed at the time.

I don't know where they met. Three days before the date on which we had decided to leave, Mummy and Daddy appeared in the stable at lunch time, and we knew at once that something had happened.

"We've been having a confab with some of the other mums and dads," Daddy said. "We've found someone to go with you. We think it'll be safer that way."

"It wasn't just us. Roderick's parents rang us up," Mummy added.

"Who've you found?" asked my brother in a wretched voice.

"There isn't anyone; not anyone nice enough," I said.

"You see you're all rather young. And even in outlandish parts like this, things can happen. Don't think we wanted to spoil everything . . ." Daddy said.

A grown-up will ruin everything, I thought. He or she will make rules; insist that we cook properly, and are in bed by half-past eight.

"He's a young chap; he does maintenance work. You may have seen him about; curly-headed, about five feet six," Daddy said.

"But can he ride?" asked Desmond in a sullen voice and with a look on his face which told me all too clearly what he was thinking.

"Yes; he hasn't ridden here; but he says he's done dressage, and he certainly knows one end of a horse from another. He's been a scout and a sea ranger too; he jumped at the chance," Daddy told us.

"Fortunately he has some leave owing to him, and can be spared next week," Mummy said.

Desmond had buried his face in Skylark's long mane. There was a long and dreadful silence.

"Well, it's better than not going at all, isn't it?" asked Daddy.

"Leslie's parents were worried too," Mummy said.

"Of course it's all right. Has he got everything?" I asked.

"What's he called?" inquired Desmond.

The first dreadful moment of disappointment was over; now we were trying to make the best of it.

"Ian Farrar. He knows a horse he can borrow and he says he's got plenty of equipment."

"Does he know where we're going?" asked Desmond, leaving Skylark to go to the window to look at the hills.

"Well, that's up to you. He's only there to keep you out of danger spots," Daddy said.

I started to groom Sandpiper again. I had been whistling the "Skye Boat Song" when Mummy and Daddy appeared, now I didn't feel like whistling any more.

"I'm sure you'll like him," Mummy said. "Hurry up and finish; it'll be lunch in ten minutes . . ."

"He may not be so awful," said Desmond when Mummy and Daddy had gone. "After all, Pony Club Camps have lots of grown-ups and everyone has a super time."

"I expect he's all right," I agreed shortly, remembering the lists Desmond and I had made; the calculations we had done, the maps we had pored over. We aren't conceited; we don't consider ourselves born leaders; but no one likes a stranger to take over when they've done all the planning.

"He may be quite an asset," Desmond said in a dismal voice. "What are we going to do after lunch?"

"Clean the tack, aren't we. It looks filthy," I replied.

But a great deal of the fun had gone from the expedition now. Desmond was gloomy; he stopped consulting maps, wouldn't discuss anything.

"How can I decide the smallest detail until I know what Ian Farrar's like?" he kept saying. And Ian was to meet us at the cross-roads on Monday at six-thirty when the ride began.

The ponies sensed our mood, and were cross too—snapping at one another, kicking when we groomed their stomachs, refusing to come when we called them.

We had telephoned the rest of the expedition—Leslie, Roddy, Jennifer and John.

"I'm afraid Mummy was to blame," Leslie said. "She got fussed when she heard that I was the eldest member of the expedition. I think she rang up your people. I can't see why parents must fuss so; but perhaps he's nice . . ."

"It's beastly, isn't it?" cried Roddy. "Is he awful? It'll spoil everything . . ."

Jennifer and John are meek children. Their father is doctor at the Base; their mother is keen on welfare work and was a nurse before she married. Their reply was typical of them.

"We're glad because Daddy *had* put his foot down. He was afraid we'd get lost in the mountains or drowned in the sea or bucked off," Jennifer said. "As it is we've got to ring up every night and give our exact whereabouts."

And as the last evening came I was suddenly glad too. Desmond and I are not Scottish. We knew nothing of mountains besides what we had learned during the last three years. Until then I had imagined sunshine, clear skies, miles of hills and mountains stretched before us. But there could be mist and fog, blinding rain, thunder. We would be shut in by the hills then, alone with the elements. Ian would be a comfort; we could turn to him and let him carry the responsibility. It was a cowardly thought, but it stayed with me all that evening, when the house was full of bustle and Desmond was suddenly alive again, checking our saddle-bags, packing the tent and sleeping-bags, while I dealt with food and polished the tack for the last time.

Mummy was suddenly nervous for our safety.

"Remember if the weather's bad you're to come back. That's a promise, isn't it?" she asked.

"Yes, but it's a red night," said Desmond. "It's going to be fine. It's my weather. You know I'm always lucky."

His enthusiasm was back and I as usual was carried away by it. We rushed about the house, packing, singing, staring at the red sun setting behind the mountains.

"I hope Jennifer and John stick it," Desmond said.

"What about Leslie?" I asked.

"She's tough."

"Thank goodness there's no Ching Poo . . ."

"He's such a ridiculous dog," complained my brother.

Miracle watched us. "You're coming; we're not going to leave you," Desmond said, stooping to stroke her long muzzle while she caressed him with her eyes.

By supper time everything was ready assembled in the kitchen.

"Our last night," said Desmond. "If only Ian is nice . . ."

"He must be; otherwise he wouldn't want to come," I reasoned.

"We'll have to lose him if he isn't," said Desmond.

We ate supper, washed up. Daddy was out. The rest of the evening seemed unbearably long.

Sandpiper and Skylark were in the stable. There was some sort of exercise going on and when eventually I fell asleep it was to the roar of planes coming in to land.

I wakened before the alarm clock went off and knew at once that this was the day Daddy had dubbed D-Day. Outside it was still dark. I sat hunched in bed remembering other early mornings—the day we had left Plymouth for Scotland, the morning when Desmond and I had gone to a gymkhana with the riding school where we had helped for so long.

This morning seemed the most exciting of all. I jumped out of bed, drew back the curtains, and at the same time the alarm clock started ringing in the passage.

CHAPTER THREE

I WAKENED Desmond. Miracle met us on the stairs. As we slung our knapsacks on our backs and picked up our saddle-bags, the sky was lightening in the east.

"It's going to be a super day," Desmond said.

We looked round the kitchen. I felt suddenly uneasy, as though I were saying goodbye to the kitchen for ever.

"Well, this is it," Desmond said. "The beginning of our holiday."

"I feel as though all sorts of dreadful things are going to happen to us," I said, following my brother out through the back door.

"Nothing more exciting than rain, I fear," replied Desmond.

Miracle knew now that she was coming; she leapt in front of us, licked our legs, smiled, frolicked like a puppy.

"Yes, you're coming," said Desmond. You're to be chief watch-dog, and don't forget it."

The ponies were lying down. They whinnied to us. It was still dark in the stable and I nearly fell over Sandpiper's hoofs.

Plymouth and Manchester seemed a long call from this early morning in Scotland; there was the lovely smell of horse and hay; soft air, a friendly silence and, in the east, a sun which rose above heathered hills instead of beyond house and factory chimney. Sandpiper opened her mouth obligingly for the bit; in the roof a bird twittered in a sleepy voice.

"I feel like a Jacobite fleeing from the Redcoats, don't you?" asked Desmond.

"I'm too happy; I feel more like Christmas," I answered.

And it was true—I felt festive; as though suddenly I had everything I had ever wanted.

We mounted in the faint light of dawn. The ponies were impatient to be gone.

"Good luck; don't forget to ring up tonight!" Mummy called from a window.

We called "Goodbye," and rode on to the road where a mist lay and trees were cobwebbed.

"We're in plenty of time," my brother said.

I turned to look at the small house, where we had lived for three years now, before we turned the first corner and it was lost to view. It was suddenly the only house I had ever really loved. Mummy and Daddy were waving from their bedroom window.

I waved and then the house was out of sight and before us lay the twisty road and adventure.

Leslie was waiting at the cross-roads; tall and slim with a straight nose, wearing a crash cap, she looked like someone waiting for hounds on a cubbing morning. We stared at her for a moment and then Desmond cried: "But she *has* brought Ching Poo." And now I could see the little Peke, bustling round Leslie's Raspberry, in the officious way we knew far too well. Rascal, a black-and-tan mongrel whom Leslie had found roaming alone on the moors, was standing by the roan pony's head. We didn't mind him, nobody did, but Ching Poo was always in some trouble or other.

"Why have you got Ching Poo?" yelled Desmond. "I thought we agreed he wasn't to come."

"He followed me. Poor little Ching, he wanted to come so badly. Och, he won't be any trouble; he hates staying at home with Nanny. He's a reformed character, really he is," answered Leslie.

"You are the limit," said Desmond. "You promised."

"But he just came," replied Leslie.

John and Jennifer arrived next on their Highland ponies Bracken and Heather. They wore jeans, crash caps, shirts and coats. They had oiled their ponies' hoofs and their tack shone brightly in the early morning light.

"Where's our escort? Hasn't he shown up yet?" called John.

"No," called Leslie.

We started to discuss our equipment. We each had a tin mug and a spoon. Desmond carried the boys' tent, Leslie the girls'. We hadn't bothered with ground-sheets, and we each carried our own sleeping-bag and a few provisions and a clean shirt. John's Alsatian had his hackles up.

"Keep him away from Ching Poo please," shouted Leslie.

"He's all right. Fearless, sit down," said John.

Hoofs clattered down the road towards us. "Am I late?" called Roddy, appearing on his little grey, Misty, followed by his West Highland, Cockade.

"I don't think so. Anyway time isn't to matter on this expedition. It's to be a holiday from rules and time," announced my brother with laughter behind his eyes.

"Well, we must know the time to ring up," Jennifer said. "We've given a solemn promise to ring up each evening before the seven o'clock surgery."

"That'll be a complication," said Desmond.

"When is Ian what's-his-name coming?" asked Leslie.

"We'll start in a minute," replied Desmond.

"Supposing we aren't near a telephone at that time?" I asked.

"But won't we be camping by then? We're going to camp near houses, aren't we? Otherwise how will we manage for water?" asked John, who had fair hair, pink cheeks and blue eyes.

"Burns," replied Desmond.

"But supposing there's a dead sheep higher up in them? Or worms?" asked John.

"Hark, hoofs! Stop yapping, Ching; Ching quiet. It must be Ian," cried Leslie.

We were silent, listening. None of us knew what Ian was really like. A van drove quietly past and then towards us came a big bay, jogging down the road like a hunt horse. I believe we all thought the same thing then—how will he manage the hills? Another moment and we could see the horse's large hoofs and then Ian, fair, curly-headed in a white polo-necked jersey, on the bay horse's back.

"Am I late? Surely not," he called, consulting his watch. "No, it's one minute to six-thirty a.m. British Summer Time. Well, it's good to be here. Pleased to meet you all, I'm sure."

He shook us all by the hand and then we started to ride along the twisting highland road, and Desmond's and my plan had suddenly become reality.

Desmond and Ian led, making plans, sometimes arguing, once unfurling a map and looking at it, perched on their mounts' withers. Ian's bay was called Tom Thumb.

The sky was blue except for a few fluffy clouds which floated like pieces of white muslin; the breeze just stirred Sandpiper's mane; the air smelt as fresh as water drawn from a mountain spring. All the world seemed mine at that moment; I had everything I had ever wanted.

"I hope his hunter can manage the hills; it's rough in places," Leslie said, riding her roan alongside Sandpiper.

"Same here," I agreed.

I saw us riding like this day after day; our friendship with one another growing deeper; the hills wilder, the scenery more beautiful.

"We *are* lucky. Think of the people who spend their lives on office stools, or behind counters; who never know this," I said. But because Leslie has rich parents and will always be able to do what she wants, or nearly, she didn't understand.

"But they like it, Sheila. They talk about their boy friends. Haven't you noticed? Och, sometimes they talk for hours while you wait," she answered.

I didn't argue. I knew she could never feel quite

as I did, because she's always lived in Scotland, never in a smoky English city. So I rode trying to engrave each moment on my memory for ever and Leslie talked:

"Och, Sheila, you look bonny with your pony tail . . . I think Ian wants us to keep to the roads. He seems nice enough . . ."

"Oh, no. We're going to ride on the moors," I said, "we want adventures."

"That's what Mummy thought. She said you two were as wild as hawks. It must be the Irish in you," answered Leslie.

I didn't intend to mar the day by argument. We had reached the famous Loch Kippen whose dark waters reflected the trees along the road, our ponies, the hills and sky. Day had come in earnest and with it the buzz of the flies rising from the bracken to attack our ponies.

Presently Ian called a halt.

"Mid-morning break," he announced. "It's ten-thirty. I think we've earned it."

We dismounted and loosened our girths.

I opened a packet of biscuits and passed it round. Leslie had a large supply of chocolate. We were still beside Loch Kippen and there was hardly a ripple on the water.

"Whew, this is fun," exclaimed Jennifer.

"Fantastic," agreed John.

"Misty's loving it," said Roddy, his arms round his half-Shetland pony.

"I should like to do this every year; summer after summer. Couldn't we? You know, keep an annual appointment year after year?" I asked.

"We'd grow older and older. What about when we were eighty?" John asked.

"It's impossible. Nothing lasts like that. There are new horizons, new countries," my brother cried, scanning the distant mountains with his restless eyes.

"Your brother will be a volunteer for space travel," said Ian, smiling at me.

"I want to ride on the moors *now*. What does everyone else think?" asked my brother, looking at Ian.

I realised then that he and Ian were at loggerheads.

"I thought that was the plan," replied Leslie calmly.

"It was the whole point of the ride," retorted Desmond.

"So we will, all in good time," replied Ian; and with that we had to be content.

The dogs lay panting, the ponies grazed, the flies buzzed incessantly. Presently we mounted and rode on.

There was a field for the ponies that night, and for a long time we stood admiring them, though Raspberry was the only one which would have looked anything in the show ring.

Ian knew the owner of the field, a rugged, fair Highlander. We had all telephoned our parents from his comfortable sitting-room.

Later Desmond was rather bitter.

"I'm not going to spend another day riding on tarmac, not for anything. The whole ride is being ruined," he said.

"The roads are a bit hard on the dogs' feet," agreed Leslie.

"We might as well be in the Midlands!" cried Desmond.

"We would get better gallops there. I like the Midlands," replied John.

"Things will be better tomorrow, you'll see," said Roddy optimistically.

Ian was fetching water when this conversation took place. Now he returned and we fell to pitching the tents; later we cooked supper on his little camping stove and drank hygienic water from the farm's supply.

"I wish I had brought my guitar," John said.

"I say, do you play one? I play the flute," cried Leslie.

We sang a few songs softly as befitted the soft Highland evening; the sky was still almost cloudless, and the air so peaceful that it was difficult to believe that any startling adventures awaited us in the length and breadth of Scotland.

When we crawled at last into our sleeping-bags, darkness was drifting over the moors and hills. We could still see the outlines of the farm, but only just.

"This is just how I imagined it would be," said Leslie.

Presently there was a moon which transformed the valley, giving to everything an air of fantasy. Far away a cow was calling to her calf, and high above us an owl hooted. Miracle lay at my feet. I wanted to explain how I felt about the whole expedition, but before the right words came I was asleep.

CHAPTER FOUR

THE next morning the farm supplied us with bacon and eggs and we ate well. Rodney's watch had stopped, my brother was impatient to be off; Ian insisted on a visit to the farm to thank his friend for the hospitality which we had enjoyed.

But at last we were riding again, our dogs yapping and tearing ahead in circles, our ponies jogging with pricked ears; only poor Tom Thumb looked wrong amid the rough scenery, like someone dressed for a night out in London, in the country on a wet Sunday afternoon.

For a long time we rode on a winding road, while the sun grew hotter and my brother angrier.

Finally he blew up. "Ian, you promised we could go on the moors today," he cried.

"Aye, you did," agreed Roddy.

"That's right," added Leslie.

"All right, but please remember it is your decision, not mine," said Ian.

So presently Roddy was leading us along a winding little path which he said would lead us to a historic glen where his ancestors were murdered in sixteen hundred and something.

And now we were all madly cheerful. Gloom vanished from Desmond's face; John and Leslie fell to discussing music, Roddy whistled Scottish songs, there was lots of laughter; our ponies looked at the hills with interest as though they were enjoying the holiday as much as the rest of us. Our dogs coursed through the heather. I gave Sandpiper her head, trusting her to pick her way over the rough ground.

We rode like that all day into the glen Roddy knew, where the mountains met the heather and there was an eeriness and a loveliness few of us had ever seen before.

Roddy still led on his little Misty, and Ian brought up the rear on Tom Thumb, who tripped and stumbled over the rough going, so that several times Ian had to dismount to lead him over some particularly bad place.

It was our last peaceful day. Only when evening came did anyone complain.

"What about telephoning? There isn't a kiosk," complained John when Roddy suggested pitching the tents, as though kiosks grew on the moors like trees.

"We must stop by a farm," insisted Ian.

"It's a wee way yet to a farm," replied Roddy.

Because the ponies were tired we dismounted to rest their backs, and started to walk. We were stiff from long hours in the saddle; an evening haze was descending, obscuring the mountain tops.

"Where's the farm, Roddy?" asked Ian presently.

"It'll be another hour before we're there," Roddy replied in his sing-song voice which somehow fits the hills so well.

In the end we pitched our tents in the glen. Ian was rather silent and kept staring into the dusk as though hoping to catch a glimpse of the farm Roddy had promised us.

Leslie and I started to tether the ponies, while the boys fetched water from a nearby burn, and Jennifer stood staring into the dusk with Ian.

We tethered the ponies to rowan trees. When we came to Tom Thumb we stood and looked at one another.

"Does he tether? I've been teaching Raspberry so she should be all right, but has Ian taught him?" asked Leslie.

"I don't suppose so. There wasn't much time for him."

"Exactly."

"We'd better wait for Ian."

"It'll soon be dark," I said.

"Ian! What about Tom Thumb. Does he tether?" called Leslie.

Ian had been checking the guy ropes. "I knew this would happen. I don't know what we're to do. If we had stopped at the farm this problem wouldn't have arisen."

"Couldn't we turn him loose? Wouldn't he stay by the other horses?" I asked.

"He might get kicked then. He isn't my horse," replied Ian.

"It's an awful responsibility," agreed Leslie.

We were sorry for Ian. We could imagine how he felt and it was mostly our fault that he was in this predicament.

"We could watch him by turns, couldn't we?" asked Desmond. "I'm not tired; I'm willing to take a long shift."

"So am I," said Roddy, who hadn't spoken to anyone since the farm-house had failed to appear.

"I don't think the girls should stay up," said Ian. "I can watch till midnight; then I'll wake one of you. I can't risk anything happening to him; he's a potential dressage horse and valuable . . ."

So we tethered Tom Thumb, tying him with Sandpiper's rope joined to his headcollar and to a tree with string so that if he did become entangled, the string would break before he damaged himself.

We were too tired to cook much of a supper; we pooled our supplies and ate baked beans, sardines, malt biscuits, chocolate, raisins and a tin of stewed steak.

"Tomorrow we *must* stop somewhere for bread; otherwise we'll be woefully short of food," Desmond said.

We had all brought tins of meat for our dogs and they fed well and after being taken to the burn for a drink, fell asleep immediately.

We were all anxious about Tom Thumb. Quite suddenly the future seemed full of unpleasant possibilities. I lay in my sleeping-bag and considered what the clouds might bring; we seemed lacking in almost everything—food, clothes, maps, elementary camping equipment. I wasn't sure now whether I wanted adventure. Wasn't riding day after day on the moors enough? There was no moon tonight; and no sound besides that made by the ponies cropping grass. At last I fell asleep—and almost immediately, it seemed, I was awakened by shouts:

"Sheila, wake up. Everyone wake up. Tom Thumb's gone!" cried Desmond.

I collected my wits. It was morning. We were camping. I scrambled out of my sleeping-bag. The dogs were barking, each trying to outdo the other. I dragged on a few clothes and blundered into Leslie fumbling with the tent flaps. I fell over a guy rope. Ian was flashing a torch.

"Oh, no," he cried. "What will his owners say? I knew this would happen if we left the roads."

"He started struggling. He broke the string almost at once; I did my best. He's terrified of the trailing rope," cried Desmond.

"You mean he's gone?" asked Ian, and there was something horribly final about those words. I think then we all saw the bay horse breaking a leg, or his neck.

There was a long silence. We couldn't see anything.

"It must be light soon," said Leslie at last.

"If only he would come when we called, as Misty does," said Roddy.

We were all together now; some with shoes, some without; John was wearing pyjamas. The dogs stood watching us hoping for a thrilling expedition.

"The girls had better go back. The rest of us can search," Ian said, without much hope in his voice.

"But that's unfair. We want to help . . ." Leslie answered.

"Someone has to stay behind," Desmond said.

"He may come back," I suggested.

So we went back to our tent, and lit a candle and found some chocolate and ate it.

"Everything's going wrong," I said.

"Supposing Tom Thumb kills himself . . .?" asked Leslie. "I wish we hadn't used string on the ends of his rope now."

"Everything's horrible. I wish we had never come," said Jennifer, searching for a handkerchief.

"We'll appreciate home more after this . . ."

I kept seeing Tom Thumb dead, bleeding from a main artery, dragging a broken leg. I too was beginning to think of everything as horrible; now suddenly there seemed no end to the disasters which might befall us. Supposing there was a fog tomorrow? Endless rain? Supposing we lost more of the ponies? If only we had stopped by a farm, how comforting it would have been then to know that there was food there, help, torches, a telephone...

Supposing our united parents sent out a search party or rescue party. They would come with stretchers and a flask of brandy and find a horse with a broken leg... poor, large, simple, big-footed Tom Thumb. And afterwards there would be the post-mortems and for ever after well-planned conventional holidays.

"It's getting lighter," said Leslie. "Look over there."

It was a slow, unfamiliar dawn which revealed the mountain on each side, the more open country beyond and never a house or telegraph wire in sight.

Sandpiper was lying down. I felt as though I hadn't slept at all.

"I hope they don't lose one another," said Leslie. And that was one more fear to add to the others. I started to wonder then why we had ever come. We could have ridden enough at home, and slept comfortably and safely in our own beds; there was really plenty to do without us walking more than a hundred yards from our cottage—we could swim, climb rocks, build castles in the sand, watch the planes coming in to land; instead we had to collect a party and start on a crazy expedition.

"I wish Daddy was here. He always knows what to do," said Jennifer.

"Desmond and I will get the blame anyway. It's our fault really; you can't get away from it . . ." I said.

I saw our return, Ian's story. No one will wish to continue if Tom Thumb's dead, I decided.

"Of course it isn't all your fault. Roddy is blaming himself. We're all to blame, including Ian, who shouldn't have brought Tom Thumb on the expedition at all," Leslie announced.

"I wish they would come back," said Jennifer, and her small face looked drawn and miserable in the early morning light.

"Will your parents panic?" asked Leslie.

"Not till this afternoon. They know you don't come to a telephone kiosk every hundred yards in this part of the world," I answered, and saw them debating what to do. "They'll probably ring up your parents," I added.

"They aren't at home. They're in Edinburgh at the moment. It'll be Nanny who's doing the keening," Leslie said.

It was really light now; and we went out and stood staring at the mountains. We had pitched our camp on grass, but around us there was high bracken, through which Tom Thumb had left a path. We could see his big hoof-prints now on the damp earth and the ground was churned where he had stood tethered.

Raspberry whinnied to Leslie and Ching Poo and Rascal ate grass and rolled.

"We'd better water the ponies," Leslie said.

And we heard voices calling, "Got him!" and a strange, sad procession came into view led by Desmond in a vest and jodhpurs. John followed still in his pyjamas, Roddy wore no shoes; Ian was the only one properly dressed. And he was talking. "I don't know how I can tell them; he's a valuable animal. It would be different if he were an old screw."

"He's sawed his heels pretty badly," called Desmond.

We could see now that Tom Thumb was moving stiffly. His headcollar was broken and the procession was so sad that even the dogs walked behind with their tails between their legs.

"Where do we go from here?" asked Leslie.

I didn't answer because I didn't know. At that moment everything had suddenly come to an end, but to what end I wasn't sure. We called, "Hallo!" and Jennifer shouted, "Oh, John, you'll catch a cold." And we walked forward to meet the little band, and somehow the hills and the mountains seemed to have defeated us. It's over, all over, I thought dismally. Now we must find our way home.

"There will be three things now. And the third will be the worst. You know how it is," I said superstitiously.

CHAPTER FIVE

We stood looking at Tom Thumb, and the sun broke through the clouds, and in the distance there was the bleating of sheep.

"Hadn't we better bathe them?" asked Leslie at last.

The bay horse hung his head; there was dried sweat on his sides; his headcollar hung in tatters. His heels were crusty with dried blood.

"I'll get the Dettol," Desmond said.

"He's finished. How shall I break it to the Macdonalds?" asked Ian.

"Do dress, John. You know Mummy hates you going about in pyjamas," cried Jennifer.

"I don't think he is finished, Ian," said Leslie in her quiet, kind voice. "He's not a show horse after all. And heels get better in time . . ."

"If only you hadn't been so insistent . . ." began Ian; and I thought, there it is, we'll get the blame. I decided then that we should have come alone, just Desmond and I, our ponies and Miracle. We could have managed without a tent, just slept under the stars, warm and waterproof in our sleeping-bags.

"Someone hold up a front hoof," said Desmond, advancing on Tom Thumb with a tin mug filled with Dettol and water.

"Och, it's Stockholm tar we should be using. Water's the worst thing," exclaimed Roddy.

"Shut up, Jennifer. I can look after myself," John said.

"Isn't powder the thing to put on them?" I asked.

"We have to put on what we have," said Desmond, straightening his back. "They'll take a week or two to heal."

"In the meantime we have to get him back to the Macdonalds. I fully expected to find breakfast ready. But the girls seem to have done nothing whatsoever," complained Ian.

"We didn't like to invade your tent," said Leslie.

The boys watered the ponies while Jennifer, Leslie and I prepared breakfast. All the fun seemed to have gone from the expedition now. Jennifer was fussing about her parents; Leslie was worried because Ching Poo wouldn't eat Good Heart tinned meat and she had nothing else to offer him. I was sorry for Tom Thumb, sorry for Ian. I was imagining our return, our feelings afterwards; our parents' reaction.

"I don't want any breakfast. I want to ride to the kiosk and ring up Mummy and Daddy," said Jennifer.

"You'll ride all the better with something in your tummy; not that there's much to eat," Leslie said.

Outside John snapped at Roddy.

"All that rot about your ancestors was wrong then. It isn't that pass at all," he said.

"As if Roddy isn't miserable enough already," Leslie murmured.

"Well, he got us into this trouble. If we had only let Ian . . ." began Jennifer.

"We would have had a deadly dull holiday," I cried.

"Don't let's quarrel," cried Leslie, and dropped the frying pan which was full of Ian's streaky bacon.

"It's gone on his sleeping-bag," I cried.

"And it's probably the Macdonalds'," cried Leslie.

"And likely to make a dressage horse," said Desmond, coming into the tent.

"It isn't funny. Hasn't Ian had enough bad luck already?" I asked, though I had an irresistible desire to giggle.

"It's covered with grease spots. Aweel, whatever can we do?" said Leslie.

"Isn't breakfast ready yet?" asked Desmond. "I've walked miles; I'm hungry."

"Can't you see it's just gone on Ian's sleeping-bag?"

"Is that all there is?"

"Almost."

Leslie was mopping ineffectually with her handkerchief. "If only Nanny were here. She knows everything," she sighed.

I said: "Try spit."

"Nothing gets grease out. You've ruined it, Leslie," said Jennifer.

"Oh, do go out, Desmond. You give me claustrophobia," I cried. "This tent is only meant for one."

I hate camping, I decided. I shall never camp again. Jennifer was frying the bacon now, neatly, efficiently and I could see her in ten years' time, a neat efficient housewife, in a frilly apron. I knew I should never be like that. My mind would be far away while toast burned, milk boiled over. I said, "Leslie, let's go out. We're only in the way."

We found Ian pacing up and down outside the tents. Desmond, John and Roddy were sitting on a hillock together.

"When's breakfast coming? My mouth's watering," cried Desmond.

"We've made some tea. Shall we start with that?" I asked.

So we sat and drank tea while Jennifer cooked, and presently Ian joined us.

"We'd better have a conference, hadn't we?" he asked.

"Yes. I think some of us should ride on looking for a kiosk and some ride slowly with you to the nearest road," proposed my brother.

"You can have my trailer, Ian. I'll give you our number," Leslie said.

"I don't know what I shall say to the Macdonalds," Ian answered.

"Can't you blame us?" I asked.

Jennifer called us then and we shared out the rest of the food. We looked at our two maps. But even Ian couldn't decide exactly where we stood. We were just marked as moors and mountains and beyond it all the sea. At last we folded them up. At least I folded Desmond's and he folded it again.

"I'll stay with you, Ian," volunteered John. "Jennifer can do the telephoning, can't you Jenny?"

"Yes, if Heather will leave Bracken," Jennifer said, pouring Leslie a second cup of pale tea.

Leslie told Ian about the sleeping-bag and the grease spots. "If you'll let me have it, I'll ask Nanny to help me get them out," she offered.

But Ian said it didn't matter; and we knew that his thoughts now were only concerned with Tom Thumb and the Macdonalds and we felt guilty.

"Wouldn't you rather have two of us with you? I'll stay if you like," I offered.

"No, John will be enough," Ian said.

We made some more plans and, then Leslie, Jennifer, Roddy, Desmond and I took down our two tents and I saddled the ponies.

We called our dogs and mounted, leaving Fearless to watch John and Ian dismantling the elegant nylon tent which Ian had borrowed, and we turned our ponies' heads towards the sun.

"Who has a nose for kiosks?" asked my brother, to which there was no answer. Behind us Bracken neighed. There were cries of "Good-bye" and "Good luck."

"I feel as though we are setting out from camp number something to climb Everest," I said.

"Instead of staring failure in the face and going home . . ." said Desmond in a bitter voice.

"If we know the way home. Where are we, Roddy?" asked Leslie.

"Och, I don't know," he said.

We remembered then that we were lost, that we could ride in circles, that there wasn't a house in sight.

"How large is this stretch of Scotland, Roddy?" asked my brother.

"Depends which way you look at it. Forty miles or more. But it meets the sea . . ."

"Won't the ponies take us home?" I asked. We dropped our reins, and with one accord they started to crop the rough grass.

"There's a road all right. It goes through Fort Angus. But it's a wee way away I'm thinking."

But we didn't believe Roddy any more. All around us there were mountains and somewhere the sea.

"We must find a kiosk," cried Jennifer, kicking Heather with her heels.

"Don't ride too fast," called Desmond.

"Steady," called Leslie.

And then the second thing happened; Heather stumbled and Jennifer went slowly over her head on to the ground.

She stood up at once, but there was blood streaming from her nose, and it took us the best part of ten valuable minutes to staunch it with our handkerchiefs; and Jennifer howled, which made her look worse than ever.

"It had to happen. It was the second thing," I announced when we had completed our first aid.

"Don't be so fatalistic," Leslie said.

"We don't want a third," cried Roddy.

We tried to raise Jennifer's spirits, but all she could think of was a kiosk. "Mummy will be so anxious," she kept saying. "We promised to ring her up if anything went wrong."

We rode on and on and nothing seemed changed, except the time, and we weren't even sure of that because only Roddy's watch was still going, and it was a relic of the twenties, passed on to him by his father, and unreliable.

"We're getting more and more lost," complained Jennifer.

"We'll reach Fort Angus soon," Roddy assured her

"I'm so tired of these beastly moors," moaned Jennifer.

"Och, why did she come then?" asked Leslie.

We ate lunch at three o'clock, briefly, almost in silence. Then we rode on.

Towards evening the path widened and suddenly we could smell the sea. Ching Poo had given up by this time and was sitting on the pommel of Leslie's saddle. Our hopes soared.

"We're getting somewhere!" cried Desmond.

"Fort Angus?" I cried.

"Och, why not?" asked Leslie.

I imagined a fishing town, nets drying, men smoking and staring out to sea; boats with Scottish names, shops.

I thought of new-made scones and my mouth began to water. I thought, there'll be butter and honey, and we'll eat and eat.

"If it's a fishing place we'll be able to buy the dogs fish," cried Leslie.

"And oats for the ponies; they deserve it," replied my brother.

"If only John and Ian were here," said Jennifer.

"They've probably reached a road by now. Perhaps they went back the way we came. I felt at one time that that was what we should have done," said Desmond. "But not now; this is much more exciting."

We could taste the salt now; our ponies were blowing, and there wasn't one of us who wasn't smiling.

"If only it's Fort Angus," Roddy said. Desmond took Ching Poo. We let our ponies walk. Then without warning we could hear the sea; another moment and it was there before us breaking against rocks and sand.

"At least there are two or three houses," said Desmond pointing.

"But there isn't a village," cried Jennifer.

The idea of scones vanished. There were no boats, no harbour, no nets drying on the sand.

But there are the houses, I thought, though they appeared strangely quiet.

"Aweel this is terrible," murmured Leslie.

"Let's investigate," said Desmond, urging Skylark into a trot.

"It isn't any use. Can't you see they're empty?" cried Jennifer.

"They can't be," replied Desmond. We rode forward slowly now, staring at the three cottages. And they stared back at us with empty broken windows, and cracked chimneys and grass growing under their doors. We stood and gazed at the sea, and suddenly the expedition wasn't a holiday any more, but a trail of disaster.

"It's all my fault, isn't it?" cried Roddy suddenly.

"No, we needn't have followed you," answered Desmond.

"What about the others?" asked Jennifer.

"What do we do now?" asked Leslie. "Where's your map, Desmond?"

Desmond spread the map on the ground, and we found the sea, and ten miles to the north of us there seemed to be a village, but between us there lay rocky hills and a steep gully.

"And there may be bogs," Leslie said.

"Why didn't we bring a compass?" asked Desmond.

"I bet Ian's got one. I wish I had stayed with John," said Jennifer.

The sea was quite calm; gulls wheeled above it. There was clean white sand and in the distance islands. Everything was remote and beautiful, without even a scrap of paper on the beach.

Cockade began barking at the sea. We let our ponies graze. We didn't speak because there seemed nothing to say—we were lost, without prospect of help. On all counts we had failed. And this was the place where the third thing was to happen.

CHAPTER SIX

"WE'D better pitch the tents," said Leslie. "It's obviously miles to the nearest town. Ching is exhausted and so are the ponies."

"What about the others?" I asked.

"I can't go on. My nose aches and aches," said Jennifer, and started to cry.

"Let's pitch the tents and Jennifer can rest for a few hours, the ponies can graze, and then we'll ride on," Roddy suggested.

"And all the faster for a break," added Leslie.

After a search we found a burn and watered the ponies. Then we tethered them, and, after watching them roll, we put up our two tents.

"I wonder how the others are faring?" said my brother.

"They're probably home by now," I answered.

Leslie helped Jennifer into her sleeping-bag.

We ate the few biscuits that we had left, and drank water from the burn.

"Well, we seem to have found some adventure," my brother said.

It was a lovely evening; golden sands met a golden sea; a few gulls pecked at shells on the sand; there wasn't a ship to be seen.

"I think some of us should explore," said Desmond. "We might find a path."

"We don't want you to get lost," I answered.

"I'll come. We need food," Roddy said.

I wanted to go; but Leslie refused to stay with Jennifer by herself, so in the end I had to stay too. Miracle went with the boys, and, when they had gone, the landscape seemed quieter than ever.

"Let's sit in the boys' tent. Jennifer's asleep," Leslie said.

"She's a bit feeble, isn't she?" I asked.

"I thought she might be. She cried at the Rally in the Easter hols, because Colonel Cauldfield called her a nitwit."

"I was afraid *you'd* be like that, having a nanny and everything. But you're not a bit," I said, wishing that I had Leslie's kindness and poise; her wonderful seat on a horse which so often made the rest of us look like beginners.

"Nannies are tougheners. You should see Nanny after my younger brothers—'there's no such word as can't'—'If you don't succeed the first time, try, try again'—'You'll never make a soldier.' Och, my tummy feels empty. How is yours?"

"Awful."

"We'd better keep talking. It keeps one's mind off food."

We talked about everything: about the feebleness of Jennifer, about Ian, about ourselves, about the ponies, about the shows we hoped one day to ride in, about school. We talked until our throats were dry and the dogs were asking tactfully for food.

Jennifer wakened with a burning forehead and we fetched her water from the burn.

"I'm sorry I'm feeble," she said.

"You're not," answered Leslie.

Jennifer's nose was very swollen, and she had a black eye.

"I wouldn't be much use on a desert island, would I?" she asked.

"Did you ever listen to Desert Island Discs? You know, what eight records would you choose, if you had a record player . . ." said Leslie.

"Listen, they're coming!" I cried.

"About time. You'd better stay lying down. You look awful," Leslie told Jennifer.

We ran outside. Roddy and Desmond waved. They were laden with shopping bags. They were singing the "Skye Boat Song".

"Everything's all right. There's nothing to worry about. We know the way to Fort Angus," Desmond shouted.

"Do you hear that? They've got food and they know the way to Fort Angus," I shouted through the tent flaps to Jennifer.

"We found 'the lone sheiling on the misty island,'" called Desmond.

"A wee cottage more like," said Roddy.

"What about a telephone?" called Jennifer, joining us.

"Nothing like that. We're thirty miles from Fort Angus. A good day's ride away," said Desmond. "Let's eat."

"But Mummy . . ." began Jennifer.

"Perhaps they'll send a helicopter to look for us," Desmond answered.

"I hope you've brought plenty for the dogs. Poor Ching."

Jennifer went back to her sleeping-bag.

"What's the matter with her?" asked Desmond. "Here, have a scone. I feel wonderful. Everything's so beautiful. I've never seen such scenery and nobody here besides ourselves. It makes one want to be a painter, doesn't it?"

"Jennifer's hurt her nose; her face is swollen a bit and she's worried," Leslie explained.

"Perhaps she's never left home before," suggested my heartless brother.

There were scones and butter, a large piece of bacon, some home-made bread, a pot of stew.

"They were a dear old couple in the cottage. They wouldn't let us pay for anything. I kept crying, 'Not so much, you can't give us all that. You won't have anything left.' But they kept saying, 'You puir children . . . you must eat. You will be getting ill,' " Desmond related.

"We will be needing a fire," Roddy said.

We gathered sticks. It was getting dark. Jennifer would only eat two scones. "It hurts to eat. Can't you see my face is swollen?" she said when we pressed her with more.

We thought she was exaggerating. We were in high spirits now. We ate and sang and saw ourselves ringing up home from Fort Angus. "And then we'll ride on and on," cried Desmond.

"If our parents let us," I answered.

"Of course they will."

"It's getting dark. Let's have a sleep before the moon comes up," suggested Leslie.

Jennifer was lying asleep when I crawled into my sleeping-bag. Because of her nose she snored loudly, and every few moments she grunted and turned over; once she ground her teeth and cried "Help!" Otherwise I could hear nothing besides the gentle sound of the sea breaking on the sandy bay.

For a time it was very peaceful lying between wakefulness and sleep, but suddenly dreadful possibilities started to rush into my mind—supposing Jennifer's nose was swelling more and more? Perhaps she was getting blood poisoning. Perhaps she had hit her head as well. Then my thoughts rushed to Tom Thumb. I saw him being sent to a horse sale, nobody wanting him.

After a time I got up and went outside.

I looked at the ponies and envied them their peace of mind, and then I saw Desmond sitting on a saddle-bag staring out to sea.

"*Great minds think alike,*" he said.

"*Dr. Livingstone, I presume,*" I replied.

"Do you think the others want to go home?" he asked.

"Why should they?"

"Well, they didn't agree when I said it would be wonderful to go on and on."

"Perhaps they were thinking about their parents," I suggested.

"It's awful to go tamely home. We'll look such failures. No one will believe in us again. And I meant this ride to prove that we could arrange things."

"Everyone makes mistakes."

"But we never succeed at anything. We're never asked to lead the ride at rallies. We're always last at gymkhanas."

Desmond is rarely sad. I had never heard him talk like this before.

"But you're good at school," I said.

"Fourth in maths, ninth in Latin . . . I say, did you see that? Look out to sea."

"Where?"

"The ship. Haven't you noticed the ship?"

"I was listening to you." I could see it now and it seemed quite near.

"In the waves. There are two men swimming," cried Desmond, standing up.

"Some people like swimming at night," I said.

"What, trawlermen?"

"Perhaps they are foreign trawlermen who like swimming by moonlight." I couldn't believe that two men bobbing like corks in the sea could mean anything to us. Desmond stood staring without speaking. Presently I said, "Well, I'm going to have a short nap. Shouldn't we start soon?"

"In about an hour. I'll wake you," answered Desmond without turning round.

Sandpiper was lying down. She looked sweet and cuddly in the moonlight, the sort of toy horse you take to bed with you when you're small.

I took off my shoes and struggled into my sleeping-bag. Jennifer was still snoring.

My head felt heavy with sleep. I shut my eyes and it seemed but a moment later that Desmond was shaking me and crying:

"Listen, it's the men. They're coming!"

"You mean the swimmers?" I cried.

"There's a boat being launched from the trawler. There's something very phoney going on." Desmond's hair had fallen over his eyes. There was no mistaking the excitement in his voice. "You see, I *was* right," he added.

I must have slept longer than I thought, because outside there was an early morning mist. The grass was cold and wet under my bare feet.

CHAPTER SEVEN

SANDPIPER was standing up. The rest of the ponies were sleeping. Roddy and Leslie joined us. And now we could hear cries in a foreign tongue, a dislodged boulder rolling down a slope. We looked at one another.

"Perhaps they're wanted men," suggested Leslie.

Our dogs stood watching, alert, their ears up. Time passed very slowly.

"What can we do . . .?"

"We ought to investigate."

"Supposing they're armed?"

"Why should they want to hurt us?"

"They may be mad."

They were coming nearer. Roddy picked up a boulder. The rest of us followed suit. We were afraid as one can be afraid in the small hours far from home.

"Och, why should they do us any harm?" whispered Roddy without conviction.

Then the dogs began to bark and into view came the two men. They were wet from the sea and had a hunted look. Their clothes told us they were foreign.

"I'm frightened. Supposing they're going to blow up Scotland," said Leslie suddenly.

"*Vrem adapost. Suntem urmariti de Rusi!*" the taller one cried.

"What language is it?" asked Desmond.

"No understand," cried Roddy.

"Perhaps they come from Mars," I suggested.

We felt calmer, but the men were growing more frantic. They threw up their hands as though appealing to God. Their faces were lined and puckered, filled with dismay.

"We must help them," said my brother.

"*Parlez-vous français?*" asked Leslie.

They shook their heads, and looked towards the mountains as though seeking help there.

"They're being chased. That's obvious. But who are they? And who is chasing them?" cried Desmond.

They pointed behind them and cried, "*Rusi, Rusi!*" They wrung their hands together and cried "*Rusi!*" and pretended to slit each other's throats.

"*Rusi, Rusi* . . . The Russians, of course. It must be!" cried Desmond.

We couldn't believe it. We gaped at the two men, while our dogs stood with their hackles up, growling in their throats.

And then we heard Jennifer calling: "*Da Da. Intrati!*" And that seemed almost more impossible, so that the episode suddenly assumed the proportions of a nightmare.

But now she was standing outside. "*Da Da. Intrati!*" she cried. Relief flooded the men's faces before they rushed into the tent.

"They are Rumanians. We must hide them," she said, and we heard her say: "*Intrati, Da,*" again.

We went in and helped to cover the two men with tack and sleeping-bags. Ching Poo kept snapping and yapping. My hands were shaking and I kept dropping things.

"I'm very sick. I'm going to lie on top of them in my sleeping-bag. Look, there's a foot showing. Take Ching away," ordered Jennifer. "They say the Russians are coming."

We went out of the tent. "I can't believe it's really happening," I said.

"You wanted adventure," said Leslie, holding Ching, who was still snarling.

"She speaks Rumanian. And I thought she couldn't do anything!" cried Desmond.

"If only we were armed," I said.

"Supposing they have machine-guns?" asked Roddy.

"They won't, why should they?" said Leslie.

"Why shouldn't they?"

"They're coming. Look over there, a cap," Desmond said, and his voice shook a little. "Oh, for a gun," he added.

"That would be fatal," murmured Leslie.

We could see heads now showing above the heather and boulders. "They're skulking," whispered Roddy.

"I'm scared," whispered Leslie.

"Don't lose your nerve. They can't just murder us for no reason," whispered Desmond.

Without thinking we had moved nearer to one another. I wished that I was six feet high and weighed twelve stone. The ponies had raised their heads. I held Miracle, who was stiff and tense, ready to spring. The moors and hills seemed quite empty, as though only ourselves, the Russians and the two unfortunate Rumanians existed in the whole world.

"Here they are," said Desmond.

I thought, why didn't we make a plan? Why didn't we split up?

"There are only three. We could defeat them," said Desmond.

"I expected ten or twelve," I answered.

"But they are armed," whispered Leslie.

And we could see revolvers bulging under their coats. They were tall and tough, and their walk was somehow relentless so that one imagined them knocking aside anything which stood in their path.

One was older than the others, with grey hair and large expressive hands.

"Men. Have you seen men? Why you up?" he asked.

Another had Mongolian features; the third was thickset, rough and ruthless in appearance.

We held our dogs with difficulty.

"They woke us. They ran away up there. We were thinking of chasing them," lied Desmond, pointing to the way we had come the day before.

I looked at the three men and was certain that they would stop at nothing. To lose the Rumanians was probably more than their lives were worth.

I thought, supposing they think it was all pre-arranged? Supposing Jennifer speaks Rumanian to them?

They were looking us up and down.

"You camp. Why?" asked the Mongolian.

"Holiday. We ride. Vacation," said Desmond.

Roddy still held a boulder in one hand. Suddenly he looked years younger, like a small boy playing a game. In contrast the Russians seemed to grow in stature. Their arms were thick and muscled. They could throw us about like puppets, I decided, and I saw us being hurled about amid the rocks and the heather.

We must have looked a strange sight with our hair tousled by sleep, me with my bare feet, Roddy clutching a boulder, Desmond defiant, Leslie holding her two dogs. I saw one smile to himself and I guessed that he had children at home. They scrutinised us, and, for a moment, there was complete silence.

Then a gull screeched. "We look," said the eldest, pointing to the tents.

I felt suddenly empty. There seemed little hope now. We had to face the worst. Were we going to fight to save the Rumanians? Leslie still held her dogs. She hadn't moved an inch. And now at last the sun broke through the early morning mist and shone on the tents, on us and on the trawler which had drifted nearer. Never was a sun less welcome. At that moment we wanted fog, not a cloudless sky.

The men spoke to each other in Russian. Two of them had their revolvers in their hands now. They were ready for a fight, and the Rumanians had no weapons, nor had we.

They spoke to one another in Russian, the eldest seeming to give the orders. One stayed outside, his revolver cocked, while the others went forward to the tent. It was a terrifying moment. Desmond stepped in front of them and said, "Sick girl inside. She falls off pony—horse," and he pretended to fall.

They laughed. They didn't trust us, that was obvious. They walked on towards the tent.

"Fetch some ponies. I'll stay with them. Be ready for a fight to the death," said Desmond quietly.

I was glad he had made the decision. My hands stopped shaking. I ran to fetch Sandpiper and Skylark, and all my tiredness had gone. I might have slept the whole night through.

Vaulting on to Sandpiper, I thought, we'll beat them somehow, even if we have to skulk for hours to get our chance; some of us can run ahead and destroy their boat, it must be somewhere in the bay. This is the most important thing which has ever happened to any of us, I decided.

The Russians were looking at Jennifer when I returned, except for the one who still stood outside, alert, ready to shoot if the need arose. I picked up a boulder and decided to hit him from behind, if he touched the trigger. I remounted Sandpiper, who was inclined to dance and snort; I put Skylark's rope under my arm, so that I had a hand free. I saw now that Roddy had collected a pile of boulders, and he had moved to one side of the tent so that he could cosh the Russians as they came out. It was difficult to believe that we were really prepared to fight; everything was so calm and quiet; there was hardly a ripple on the sea, hardly a cloud in the sky; no wind stirred the heather.

The Russians were talking to Jennifer.

"Me children," said one, and then after a pause: "girl like you."

The other said, "Your face," and started to laugh.

Desmond cried, "She has a headache. Please, don't talk so loud. Bad head." I knew he was suffering agonies of suspense. He was trying to get them out, but they went on talking and laughing.

"Oh, sweets. Oh, thank you very much," said Jennifer.

"Och, they will be there for ever," complained Roddy.

Leslie was sitting on the heather holding all the dogs. Sandpiper started to paw the ground; Skylark's rope slipped from under my arm and I had to dismount to retrieve it.

The eyes of the Russian outside never left the tent, his finger remained on the trigger of his revolver. Flies were buzzing now in the heather. Morning had really come. "This is awful," muttered Roddy.

"Are they still talking?" I asked.

"They keep giving her sweets and one has produced a snapshot of his little girl," Roddy said.

Finally we heard them say "Good-bye."

They came out and the one outside put his revolver back inside his coat and they stood and talked, ignoring us completely. I could hear Desmond muttering to Jennifer; then he too appeared. "Keep hold of the dogs whatever you do," he said to Leslie in barely audible tones. And to me: "Keep alert, Sheila. Things can still happen."

We must have looked suspicious to the Russians with boulders in our hands, with dogs straining against their collars, and two ponies standing ready for action.

But having children of their own, they may have suspected we were playing a game; anyway after a discussion between themselves, the eldest said, "Thank you. We look at other tent."

We let them go, and again the third one stood outside with his revolver cocked. We could hear them moving our sleeping-bags around. Miracle snarled. Sandpiper and Skylark fidgeted. I thought, it's all right, everything's going to be all right.

They came out of the boys' tent, but still they didn't go. They stood and looked at us and then out to sea and, following their eyes, I saw that beyond the lonely bay there were half a dozen ships. I felt a sudden rush of terror then and suddenly everything seemed too big for us to handle alone. I wanted grown-ups to take over, coast-guards, the British Navy, the police. But around us were the hills, the mountains and desolate coast—there was no help anywhere.

I looked at Desmond and he turned his thumbs down. Roddy had taken Cockade from Leslie. He stood with his terrier and in one hand he still held a large boulder. Leslie seemed to grow smaller the longer she gazed out to sea. But she had a determined look about her too, and I knew suddenly that in spite of the ships we were still ready to fight. I thought, the Russians could kidnap us and nobody would know for days. They would search the moors; perhaps the ponies would return home, perhaps our dogs. There would be a tremendous search then with police and planes, perhaps the army too, but no one would ever discover what had really happened, perhaps not for years. The thought made me feel funny to the marrow of my bones; there was a shiver down my spine. Is this really happening to us, I thought.

The Russians looked at us again, as though trying to decide whether we had the brains to trick them. Cockade, seeing their eyes on Roddy, started to yap furiously. And then far out to sea a ship's hooter sounded.

I think we all jumped, even the Russians. They spoke to one another, then turned to us.

"Those are our ships. If you see ze men, let us know. We will give you money. Yes?" said the eldest.

"Yes, fine," said Desmond and he seized the Russian's hand and shook it.

"Good-bye and good luck." They shook our hands and then, to our dismay, opened the tent flap and called "Good-bye" to Jennifer. Then at last they trudged away, their eyes scanning the hills, while out to sea the ships seemed to have drifted nearer, so that now we could see the unfamiliar flag they flew.

CHAPTER EIGHT

For a moment we were stunned by relief. "They're going," said Desmond after a silence, in incredulous tones.

We were suddenly filled with triumph. Then we started to see the problems ahead. How long would the ships stay watching us? Had they men with field-glasses trained on our two tents? Would more Russians land? Or had more already landed? For ages we stayed exactly where we were, talking in whispers.

We were afraid the Russians were watching us from behind rocks.

"We looked guilty enough," whispered Desmond.

"And as frightened as the Rumanians. I'm still shaking," whispered Leslie.

"Our whole set-up must have seemed suspicious," I said.

"Supposing another search party turns up?" asked Leslie.

"Sooner or later they must give up the search," replied Desmond.

We began to talk more loudly.

"Och why? The Rumanians may be of tremendous political importance," replied Rodney.

"They must be if they were on a Russian ship," said Desmond.

"Perhaps they were part of a delegation," Leslie suggested. "And they didn't like Russia and decided to escape to the West."

"Wasn't Jennifer marvellous?" I said.

"We misjudged her," replied Roddy.

"She's got twice our brains," said Desmond.

"I hope her father isn't a spy. It seems so funny that she should know Rumanian," Leslie said.

"Perhaps she has a Rumanian relation," I suggested.

"A Rumanian grandmother, why not?" agreed my brother. "Whoever heard of a doctor being a spy?"

"Well, he's in a jolly good place to spy. The base is pretty hush-hush after all," Leslie insisted.

"Only one bit of it," replied Desmond.

"Surely she wouldn't have saved the Rumanians if her father was a Communist," I said.

We released our dogs and they ran backwards and forwards through the heather, their noses to the ground, tracking the Russians.

We called them back.

"How are we going to get the Rumanians away?" I asked.

"We'll have to ride by night, tonight," cried Desmond, his face relaxing. "It's fantastic, isn't it? Think of the story we'll have to tell when we get back!"

"If we do get back. Supposing they are murderers?" asked Leslie.

"The Russians would have told us," replied my brother.

"Tonight is such hours away," I complained. I wanted to be on the move again. I didn't like the thought of waiting for hours with the Russian ships watching us from the sea.

"Yes. I agree with Sheila. Let's move soon," said Leslie. "Otherwise we may have trouble with another Russian search party."

"We must have cover of some sort. Probably they're

watching us now from the ships. We can't risk a fight," replied Desmond.

Let's talk to Jennifer. She should have a say," I suggested. I wanted to see the Rumanians again; already I had forgotten what they looked like.

"Och, they must be stifling," cried Leslie.

"We'd better have a ride round first. There may be men with guns trained on us from behind boulders. We simply can't take risks. I'm determined that we shall reach Fort Angus with the Rumanians alive," said my brother, vaulting on to Skylark.

He and I cantered for a mile or more, bareback, our ponies in headcollars.

"This seems a long call from town life, doesn't it?" called my brother once.

"A thousand million miles," I replied.

I was suddenly happy. I felt that we were belonging truly to our time, that this was what life was really like for thousands of people. Desmond seemed suddenly to have grown up.

He halted Skylark. "Oh, for a pair of field-glasses. I wish I knew what was going on in those ships," he said.

We could see them and that was all. Beyond them were a few small islands, and then the Atlantic stretching away until it met the summer sky.

"It seems impossible that this is happening," I said.

"You mean everything is so peaceful?"

"Yes, and beautiful. Why do humans have to be so horrible? Why can't they leave the Rumanians alone?"

"I don't know. I can't see anything suspicious. We'd better go back, don't you think?"

We trotted back. Leslie and Roddy hadn't moved.

"There doesn't seem to be anyone about," reported Desmond.

We tied up our ponies. "Aren't they quiet? They must have great patience," I said, alluding to the Rumanians.

"They're frightened. One can see it in their eyes, like rabbits pursued by a ferret," said Roddy.

"None of us really knows what fear is," said Leslie. "Not the fear of being hunted, or running for your life. But supposing they are really criminals?"

We rushed into the tent then, imagining Jennifer knocked senseless.

But nothing had changed.

"I thought you were never, never coming. They haven't stirred. I hope they're not suffocated," Jennifer said. Her nose had swollen more; she was grotesque. I remember thinking, she's the hero of this expedition, before we started to remove the pile of tack and sleeping-bags which concealed the two men.

Our dogs had followed us. They stood now with their hackles up, growling. Presently Ching started to yap and run backwards and forwards across the tent. "Ching. Och, Ching. Stop it. Hold your tongue," cried Leslie.

I thought we would never reach the men. I imagined them suffocated, and us transporting two dead men instead of two live Rumanians to Fort Angus.

But at last we revealed a worn shoe, then a canvas trouser leg. They were all right, but for an hour they wouldn't move at all for fear the Russians would return. They insisted on us replacing the tack. The dogs were mystified. It was very hot now. Sweat ran off our faces.

"They'll die of heat under all that," Desmond said. We all went outside.

"Jennifer, you were superb. Absolutely fantastic.

How on earth do you know Rumanian? Your parents are English, aren't they?" asked Desmond.

"You saved the day, and the Rumanians," I added.

"I wish those ships would go. Och, I'm getting a thing about them. It's as bad as having a neighbour looking at you over the garden wall all the time. And I'm not used to neighbours," said Leslie.

"We had a Rumanian living with us before we came here," explained Jennifer. "She was sweet. She became John's and my nanny, more or less. Her parents were both dead, and she was born in England; her mother was English, too, so she claimed British nationality I think. Anyway somehow or other she got out of Rumania after the war. Daddy heard about her. She hadn't any money at all then. So she lived with us and because she was homesick she taught us Rumanian, not much, but a bit. I'm interested in languages, it's what I'm going in for if I get the chance," Jennifer continued. "But Nanny's really a very nice person. She was terrified of everything when she first came. For ages, whenever she saw a policeman she used to hide on the other side of the road, or go into a shop and buy something. And when one came once about Fearless's licence, she was quite certain he had come for her. She hid in the cupboard under the stairs. It was funny."

"Where is she now?" I asked, imagining a stocky nanny in a large apron.

"She got married last year. She lives in London now," said Jennifer.

"Perhaps she'll be able to help these two later," I suggested.

"Thank goodness we have you with us, Jennifer, that's all I can say," exclaimed Desmond.

"But what are we going to do now?" asked Leslie.

"Eat," said Desmond.

We finished the stew. There wasn't much left. We were still hungry afterwards. We took scones to the Rumanians.

But they wouldn't raise their heads. They had picked up the word "No" and they kept muttering, "No, no, *Rusi, Rusi,*" until finally we tied up the tent flaps and left them in peace.

We screwed up our eyes and looked at the ships. "Surely they will go soon," I said.

"They have to sail with the tide," Roddy answered.

"What will we be doing next?" asked Leslie.

We had stopped looking over our shoulders. We sat down in the heather.

"We must have a council of war," said Desmond. "In my opinion our only chance is to ride under the cover of darkness, between dusk and the moon rising. Otherwise we can be seen saddling the ponies, taking down the tents, and by the time we leave a boat will have been dispatched . . ."

"Will the Rumanians be riding then? We haven't enough ponies to go round. That's the pity of it," Roddy said.

Miracle climbed on to my knee. I tried to imagine us finding our way across the moors in pitch darkness. It wouldn't be easy.

"I suppose two of us can ride on one. Sandpiper's strong enough," I replied.

"Supposing the Rumanians can't ride. What will we be doing then?" Leslie asked.

"You'll have to find that out, Jennifer. Do you know the verb 'to ride' in Rumanian," Desmond asked.

"No, but I know horse."

"At least the Russians haven't got ponies too," I said.

"My watch has really stopped this time. Will any of you be knowing the time?" asked Roddy.

My watch said twelve o'clock but it had stopped too. Nobody else had wound theirs in hours.

"It's immaterial really, isn't it?" asked Desmond. "Let's get on with our plans. Does everyone agree we ride as dusk turns to night?"

"Yes. But I wish Ian were here. He would know how to signal for help," Jennifer said.

"Where from? There is no help," replied Desmond.

"I don't suppose we would be here if he had stayed with us. You all despised him, but . . ." began Leslie.

"Well, I'm glad to be here, I wouldn't miss this for anything in the world," cried Desmond, jumping to his feet.

Miracle left my knee; the ponies raised their heads. "Don't you see the opportunity we have?" cried Desmond.

Ching started to yap. "Stop it, Ching Poo, Ching," shouted Leslie.

"Some of us should go ahead. That will be the best plan. It may muddle the Russians. We can meet at the old people's wee house," suggested Roddy, whose face had turned red in the sun.

"I will go with you, Roddy. Ching Poo had better take the first part slowly, if he's to make the journey at all," Leslie said.

"You mean we're to follow you up. It's not a bad idea," said Desmond.

"Yes, you or Sheila had better ride Raspberry," replied Leslie.

"Sandpiper and Skylark are the only two up to the Rumanians' weight, so I suppose they'll have to ride them," I said.

"If they can ride," answered Leslie.

"I hope the house has a telephone," Jennifer said.

"Losh, nothing like that. This isn't a London suburb," cried Roddy.

"Poor Mummy," sighed Jennifer.

"She'll have a fit when she sees your nose," I said.

"We can always say the Russians did it. That would cause an international scandal," said Desmond.

"You musn't be seen leaving. Then, when we pack up and ride away they may just count our heads, if they can see anything at all from their ships," Desmond told Leslie and Roddy.

We all looked out to sea then and the small fleet of ships was still there, swaying gently on the calm sea, looking like ships in a picture.

"Can you explain our plans to the Rumanians, Jennifer?" asked Desmond.

"I don't know. I'll try . . ."

"I suppose we'll carry weapons of some sort," I said.

The ships made me uneasy. Supposing they had men posted all along the coast? They might be waiting for us in the dark. Then we would have to trust in our ponies' speed, and supposing the Rumanians were poor horsemen? I imagined the rapid cracking of a machine-gun . . . the hills suddenly alive with Russian seamen, who would shout "Stop!" or the equivalent in Russian, and then they'd fire: and there would be flashes of light in the dark, and we'd topple off our horses, and there'd be no one there but the Russian seamen, and the two frightened Rumanians, doomed to years of imprisonment. I wasn't ready to die. I longed now for reinforcements, but around us were the hills, and in the bay the ships; we had to rely on our wits and our steeds.

Jennifer went back to the Rumanians and Roddy and Desmond stood outside while she talked, for fear the Rumanians might turn out to be bad characters after all.

Leslie, Jennifer and I watered the ponies; then we groomed them, and checked their shoes, and tied them up, so that they wouldn't eat too much before we started on our ride.

I told Sandpiper that she was to carry a frightened man. "You must look after him, even if he can't ride at all. It's a matter of life and death. You must watch for boulders; whatever happens you mustn't shy or falter," I told her, and saw the Rumanians falling, us turning back; I felt the eeriness of the hills at night and I thought we were mad. But somehow we must succeed. Life seemed suddenly like a film, like the Scarlet Pimpernel, like a host of exciting books, but not like life at all.

I looked out to sea and thought of the terrified men who were afraid to move from the tent, and I knew that we were fighting something big, far bigger than ourselves. I put my arms round Sandpiper's neck and she nuzzled my back, and I thought, we'll fight if necessary; a moving horse is a difficult target, we'll spread out. They can't shoot us all. Then I fell to wondering what Rumania was like. Were the people like Italians? The French?

Leslie was beside me then and she said, "Do you think Jennifer will make the journey?"

"Why not? Her spirit has returned . . . We were all wrong about her, weren't we?" I asked.

"Brains and stamina don't seem to go together. And she's hardly eaten for two days."

"She ate some stew this morning."

Leslie shrugged her elegant shoulders. "Well, she's your pigeon . . . as Nanny would say."

She called her dogs and I realised now that it must be afternoon, half-way to dusk. Ching Poo was limping, and Leslie picked him up and went away saying, "Poor Ching, poor little Ching."

There wasn't a ripple on the sea; the sky was clear, the night promised to be fine and warm. By tomorrow morning we should have reached Fort Angus—God willing.

The police could ring our parents then . . . I gazed at the scenery as though looking at it for the last time; then I went back to the tents.

CHAPTER NINE

"YES, I think they can ride. I think one's called Vintila and the other Ioan. They come from near Bucharest; that's the capital," Jennifer said.

We hadn't eaten. It must have been three o'clock. Flies buzzed in the heather. It was our last discussion before Leslie and Roddy set off together.

"What if you don't turn up?" asked Roddy.

"One had better wait, the other go on and fetch the police," Desmond said.

We were in deadly earnest now. Tom Thumb's scraped heels and Jennifer's fall were nothing compared with what lay ahead. The Russian ships were still in the bay.

Vintila and Ioan had eaten the last of our scones; there was still a piece of smoked bacon in reserve.

"Give Raspberry plenty of rein, Sheila," Leslie said, standing up.

"Misty is easy; she goes like a polo pony over the heather; it's nothing to her," said Roddy with pride.

For some reason they shook our hands and we said things like "Godspeed" and "Have courage" and "Good-bye." We felt suddenly that we might never see them again and none of us spoke as they trudged away.

For a long time we watched them skulking from boulder to boulder, then Desmond said: "Do the Rumanians understand exactly what we're doing, Jennifer?"

"I hope so, but they're jolly frightened."

"They were lucky finding us; and really it's marvellous for us," said Desmond with a smile.

"If we succeed . . ."

"Well, it's a chance of a lifetime at any rate," said my brother.

"It's a bit like ten little niggers—now there are only three," said Jennifer.

"We might have asked the Russians the time."

"Is it the same as ours?"

We went on talking though I think all our thoughts were with Roddy and Leslie, or riding already through the night, or at home with our anxious parents. And still the ships were in the bay, and the Rumanians remained in the tent partly covered, and our dogs watched us, waiting, knowing that something was about to happen.

"It must be tea-time now," said Jennifer wistfully. And we thought of tea, of iced cakes, of buttered scones, and toast, of birthday cake, of cream teas in Devon and of Cornish splits in Cornwall. Then, quite suddenly, we weren't hungry any more and the sky was darkening.

"We'll take this tent down first," said Desmond.

We felt as though all the world was staring at us as we pulled up the pegs. "Supposing they're just waiting for this moment?" I asked.

"Who are *they*?"

"The Russians . . ."

"We'll put Vintila and Ioan up, and I'll ride with them. You girls can roll up the tent and follow. I'll go slow, unless anything happens . . ." my brother said.

We fumbled with the pegs; I looked over my shoulder but there was nothing there. Miracle began to growl.

The dusk was suddenly full of weird sounds. Our ponies stood waiting with pricked ears.

"I wouldn't be a spy for all the money in the world," announced Jennifer.

"What are you going to do with all your languages then?"

"Teach. Be an interpreter. Look after tourists."

We folded the tent.

"I wish those ships would go. It's as though there were hundreds of eyes watching us," I said.

I felt shaky at the knees, but I knew once I was mounted that would vanish. Then I started to think of the things which could go wrong. Supposing Raspberry refused to stand still? After all, she didn't know me; and Misty, Skylark and Sandpiper would be disappearing ahead of us in the dusk.

Supposing we couldn't get the Rumanians up? They might have misunderstood Jennifer's Rumanian, which was hardly better than my French. We would be easy targets then...

"They give me the creeps," Jennifer agreed, and her voice was small again, and her face pale in the dusk.

"Would you rather go on ahead with the men?" asked Desmond.

"No, you know the way. We can follow. We'll be all right, won't we, Jennifer?" I asked.

She said "Yes," and we went into the other tent and fetched out our sleeping-bags and tack and tried to explain to the men that we were about to leave. They looked unshaven, tired and hollow-eyed, like people who haven't slept for a long time. But there was something nice about their faces too; even if they didn't smile, it was easy to imagine them laughing at some other time.

They kept saying "*Multumesc*" which Jennifer explained was "Thank you," and they patted Miracle and asked Jennifer her name.

We saddled and bridled our ponies, and looked out

we were mounting, and suddenly there was moonlight and nothing ahead but the same kind of scenery for a good many miles.

The ponies were in a hurry. Raspberry threw up her head, and I could hear Jennifer whispering, "Steady, Heather, steady."

We could see the hills clearly in the moonlight. Above us there seemed a million stars; and away on our left the derelict cottages suddenly seemed lit. Supposing they're inhabited by Russians? I thought, before I realised that it was the reflection of the moon on the few remaining window panes which caused the illusion.

"Can you see a path?" called Jennifer.

I was leading—it was Raspberry's choice.

"Sort of."

"I can't see Desmond," cried Jennifer.

"Nor can I."

I wanted to gallop, but the ground was too rough. Although there was moonlight, there were shadows too, sudden patches of darkness where a hill hid the moon. There were boulders and rolling stones, sudden dips, holes. I was afraid of marking Raspberry, of facing an irate Leslie when everything was over and we were home again. If we ever were home again. Suddenly it seemed impossible. How could we find our way to Fort Angus? We would die of starvation before that, fall off and crack our heads on rocks, or be shot in mistake for the Rumanians. I was suddenly cold; and I wished that we had never set eyes on Vintila and Ioan.

"I can't see the sea now," called Jennifer, who suddenly seemed feeble, as she had before she spoke Rumanian and stunned us into admiration.

"Nor can I." Raspberry was pulling, ducking her

head and then throwing it up. It's my hands, I thought. I can't ride like Leslie. And then there was the *crack crack* of gunfire, and it was like a sudden blow waking one from dreams to reality. Suddenly nothing mattered except that we were riding for our lives. We forgot the

rocks and boulders under our horses' hoofs; we gave them their heads, drummed their sides frantically with our legs, and they responded.

I think Jennifer called "Help!" involuntarily, just because she is the sort of person who does call "Help." I forgot about the path. I only knew that we had no weapons, that Miracle had gone with Desmond, that we had only ourselves to save.

And there were still the same maddening hills on each side of us; the same miles of moor, and no house save the two deserted cottages we had left behind.

We galloped, waiting for another burst of gunfire, and I started to think. "Supposing they'd shot Desmond? What about Roddy and Leslie? The Russians might be capable of anything." There seemed little hope then of anything but disaster for any of us, and yet I felt a strange uplift, as though this was really life and everything which had gone before was soft and over-civilised by comparison.

CHAPTER TEN

The hills didn't change. Presently I had to pull up Raspberry, who had out-distanced Heather. I had a chance to look around; there were plenty of boulders, enough to conceal an army. Night seemed to have come in earnest; at least there was the atmosphere of night in the air, and far away an owl hooted. I couldn't see a path; we seemed to have fled across heather, through deep bracken; possibly we had ridden in a circle, and our poor tent would suddenly come into view and the two cottages and the bay full of ships. Anything might happen then—there might be Russians waiting for us by the tent; or the ship might have sailed, or steamed, rather, away.

It was agony to stand waiting for Jennifer. I was a sitting target. "Come on, hurry," I shouted.

"I'm coming as fast as I can. Heather isn't as fast as Raspberry. I can't help it."

The ponies were sweating; our reins were white and

slippery; my jodhpurs were wet, and the salt from Raspberry's sides stung my legs.

"I don't see the old people's cottage," cried Jennifer.

"We're lost. Come on, ride. We're riding for our lives," I said, and at that moment a curlew flew out of the heather with a mournful cry, frightening us into action.

Our ponies needed no urging. In my experience horses always do rise to an occasion; certainly Raspberry seemed ready to gallop until she dropped.

We galloped on and the night was full of strange sounds, and I saw, not the hills, but Desmond shot, lying somewhere in the heather with a blood-soaked shirt. I saw myself breaking the news to Mummy and Daddy, the shocked silence, our tears afterwards. I saw the cottage without Desmond; the empty bedroom, Skylark unridden, Miracle watching for him, waiting, unable to understand. I saw it all so clearly that everything was hidden by my tears; they streamed down my cheeks on to Raspberry's elegant pulled mane, they trickled down her wet shoulder on to the hateful heather which somewhere was stained scarlet with my brother's blood.

Peace and home seemed then to belong to another life. Nothing would ever be the same again without Desmond. I should hate Scotland, I should never look on her high and heathered hills without horror.

"Hurry," I called back, "Desmond is hurt!"

"How do you know?" I had to wait for Jennifer.

"I know because he's my twin," I screamed.

"Galloping in circles won't help," said Jennifer suddenly beside me. I looked at her and she looked so frail, so tired, like someone sick in hospital, that I was sorry I had screamed.

"I'm afraid. I know he's hurt. It's awful being a twin;

you don't know what it's like. I know he's hurt, that's all."

I started to cry again. "I'm sorry. I'm all to pieces," I said.

"I know. I felt like that about John. But he isn't a twin and we hadn't met the Russians then, and so it wasn't nearly so bad."

"We must find the path . . ."

I let Jennifer take over. She seemed quite calm. She sat on her pony murmuring about east and west, where the sea was and where the moon. Raspberry stood blowing, and I thought, supposing I've broken her wind? But at that moment it didn't matter; at that moment nothing mattered but Desmond lying somewhere in the heather.

Jennifer led more soberly. "I think we've left the Russians behind, if it was really them shooting at us . . ." she said.

"I don't care about them. I only want to find Desmond.

"That means riding towards the cottage, or the lone shieling or whatever your brother called it."

"Yes, I suppose so." I felt exhausted. I let Raspberry follow Heather, and presently she stumbled and after that she was lame. I rode her for a time, convincing myself that my brother mattered more than Leslie's beautiful four-hundred-guinea roan pony, but at last I couldn't bear her limp any longer. "Jennifer, Raspberry's lame," I called. I dismounted. And there seemed nothing left but to give into the fate which had dogged us for so long. "She really *is* lame," I added. "We may as well give up. This is the end, isn't it?"

We dismounted and stood looking at the roan pony.

"If only those wretched Rumanians hadn't appeared. We were going to be all right," I said. My teeth began to chatter. I looked around and saw that the hills had changed; the ground was flatter, and not far ahead there were black-faced sheep standing together in a huddle watching us.

"Somehow we've all mismanaged everything," I said.

"But we can't give up. We can't just leave Raspberry. We'll have to take it in turns to walk, that's all. I can't see why Daddy hasn't sent out a search party by now . . ." Jennifer complained.

"Perhaps he has. Perhaps planes are looking for us. We can't have been easy to see, most of the time we've been between hills."

"There's our tent; it's white . . ."

I think we both felt very lonely suddenly; as though we had been abandoned, left to fend for ourselves, as though no one cared. It was a silly, uncalled-for feeling; but we were hungry and exhausted and self-pity came easily. Then I remembered Desmond.

"We can't waste time. In the end we must reach somewhere," I cried.

We took it in turns to ride Heather, and gradually there were more sheep, and we stopped to drink at a trickling burn, and slowly the moonlight faded and dawn came grey and cold above the hills.

Our feet were wet with dew and we were so cold that now our teeth chattered incessantly. And Raspberry lagged; she looked pitiful and tired, her head hung, her usually beautiful tail which she carried like a banner was now sticky with dirt and sweat and dragged between her legs; her flanks were hollow. And it was another day. We couldn't even remember which day it was. But at least walking had become easier; and the moors suddenly seemed more civilised. One could imagine shepherds now driving sheep with a dog, people shooting grouse.

"It's a pity Desmond took the map," Jennifer said.

It was ages since we had said anything except, 'Your turn now . . .'

"Yes," I said, and wondered where it was at this moment. Everything by this time seemed blunted by tiredness. When I was riding it was difficult to keep awake; when I was walking I just put one foot in front of the other.

"We'll reach somewhere soon. The others may have joined up by now. Perhaps they've already reached Fort Angus." Jennifer's voice was hoarse, I realised. She was walking again. From the back of Heather, she appeared small, and her shoulders drooped, and she walked with her head down.

And then suddenly she seemed to come to life. "Look, look, over there!" she cried. "Look, wires, telephone wires. . . ."

We started to run then, pulling our ponies after us. I saw us telephoning the police, doctors, home. After that we would wait to be rescued and fed. Raspberry dragged and limped, and we passed more sheep, and gradually the wires grew nearer. Jennifer was a fast runner, and several times she had to wait for me.

"They probably lead to a house. We can follow them and telephone from there," she cried.

But I knew they might lead miles before they reached anywhere. My legs were aching; my jodhpur boots felt like lead on my tired feet. I think I would have given up if Jennifer hadn't kept running. And then suddenly she stopped. "Oh, look, oh, Sheila!" she cried.

In front of us was a gorge, below us a shallow river. And before us wire, four strands of it, stretching across the moor for miles. We couldn't even jump it on the ponies. One of us could with difficulty continue on foot, but to where? I loosened Raspberry's girths and sat down, and for a long time we were silent, while our ponies searched among the heather for the rough hill grass which grew there.

"We can't give up," I said at last. I left Raspberry, and walking forward I wrenched at one of the posts, threw my shoulder against it, beat it with a boulder, but nothing happened. I kicked the strands of wire, twisted them, found a sharp stone and sawed with it. I didn't even dent them.

"I can't see how we lost sight of Desmond . . ." said Jennifer.

"It was the firing. Perhaps he heard it too," I answered.

We remembered the bacon in my saddle-bag and when we had eaten it we began to feel better.

"You know, we haven't examined Raspberry properly yet," I said. I ran my hand down her tendon; it was cool, without any suspicious swelling.

"Perhaps it's her shoulder," suggested Jennifer.

I stood back and stared at Raspberry. She looked like a horse which had been hunted hard all day. Heather was only slightly run up, but Raspberry's stomach line was like a greyhound's.

"We're quite mad. We haven't looked to see whether there's a stone in her hoof yet," Jennifer said.

I picked up her hoof and there between the frog and the wall was a small, sharp flint.

"And we've dragged her all these miles. What's the matter with us?" I cried.

Jennifer got up and looked over my shoulder.

"Can you pull it out?" she asked.

"It's so elementary, the sort of thing you know when you take D Test," I cried, exasperated.

We couldn't move the flint; every step must have wedged it firmer; and Raspberry had taken a good many limping steps.

Then I remembered my knife with the hoof pick in it, and after a struggle I got the flint out.

"Now we can both ride."

"If she's sound."

"We've been so incompetent. We're hopeless," I said. I led Raspberry forward.

"It's all right. She's sound," said Jennifer.

"Where do we go from here?" I asked.

"I don't know. My head's aching fit to burst."

"It's going to rain soon," I said, looking at the sky. The air was growing heavy. "Supposing there's a fog?" I saw us roaming for ever round and round the same piece of desolate moor, engulfed by fog, growing weaker each moment. "We *must* go on," I cried.

"Where? Shouldn't the ponies rest? And we've eaten, but they haven't," replied Jennifer.

But I couldn't wait; there was still Desmond to find. "They can eat when it's dark, or too foggy for us to ride any more, or when we get home, if we ever get there..."

I mounted Raspberry, pulled up her girths, found my handkerchief and wiped her sticky reins. The sweat had dried on her coat in a thick crust. We looked disreputable now; even Jennifer, who usually looked meek and well-washed. There was a mixture of dirt and tears on our faces; our hands were grimy from sweaty reins, our jodhs. and jeans stuck to our legs; our hair was tangled.

"We must reach somewhere soon," I said, but I didn't believe the words. We could ride for ever without reaching anywhere. But our short rest had given us more hope. Jennifer mounted and we followed the tumbling river, while the sky grew greyer and the air heavier. And every moment our surroundings grew flatter and there were more sheep. The wires had disappeared across the other side of the river. We passed a ruined chapel and saw in the distance a cairn on a hill-top.

We seemed to be nearing civilisation.

"We'll have to send a search party back if we reach a town. Do you think they'll believe us?"

"I dont' know . . ." replied Jennifer. She was riding limply, like someone in a dream, or half asleep.

"And we'll eat and eat; the police will feed us," I cried hopefully, trying to cheer up Jennifer. "There'll be meat and three veg. and Yorkshire pudding and ice-cream . . ."

"If only we could ring up home . . . Supposing John's hurt?"

"He's all right. He's with Ian . . ."

She swayed slightly. "Are you all right?" I asked, suddenly concerned for her.

I drew rein, but too late. Very slowly she toppled off into the heather. I dismounted and knelt beside her and the ponies cropped what grass there was, and everything seemed very still. I thought of the town we might have reached quite soon; of people running to greet us. I found Jennifer's pulse. My watch had stopped a long time ago. I counted instead, and decided that she was suffering from lack of food and exhaustion. Her pulse seemed very slow at any rate. I took my jersey out of my saddle-bag and put it over her. I didn't know what to do. I looked at Jennifer and remembered how we had despised her; I remembered her talking Rumanian. And now she had ridden and walked until she passed out through exhaustion. I realised then that one should never judge people. I loosened the ponies' girths, took their bits out of their mouths and tethered them to the boulders which lay about.

Then I sat down and tried to think.

CHAPTER ELEVEN

I SAT for a very long time. I could see no way out of my predicament. I could leave Jennifer and ride on alone in search of help, but it might be hours before I reached a town; the fog might come down: we might never find her again. I could wait for her to come round, but supposing she didn't come round? I could tie her to Heather's back with the tethering ropes, but was I strong enough to lift her into the saddle? I was unnerved by our recent disasters; I hadn't the courage to make a decision. I sat waiting for something to happen; and presently something did happen.

First of all Jennifer turned over and said, "Where am I?"

I knelt down beside her. "We're on the moors," I answered. "Don't you remember?"

"Oh, I thought that was all over. We're still lost then? I fainted. I remember now . . ."

"Yes."

"What's the time?"

"Don't you remember, we let our watches stop days ago." (It seemed more like years.)

"And we haven't any food and Raspberry's lame; and we found a river . . ."

Jennifer shut her eyes as though she didn't wish to face our circumstances.

"Our only hope is to ride on. Do you think you can?"

"Yes, in a minute or two."

I tightened the ponies' girths, put their bits back in their mouths. We seemed to have wasted a great deal of time. It would soon be afternoon, I decided. And I didn't want to spend another night on the moors. This time without a tent, and without food.

"Are you ready?" I asked.

"In a minute." She stood up; her jeans had slipped down nearly to her hips. I tightened my own belt a notch.

"We'll soon reach Fort Angus," I said with a firmness I didn't feel.

"We hope," said Jennifer. "I hope the others are there. I hope they're all right. I hope so many things and probably none of them will happen."

"You're tired, that's all," I said.

She leaned against Heather. "There's a fog coming, or a mist at any rate. We must go on. It's a matter of survival," I told her.

She said, "Yes. All right. I'm all right. It's just my nose. It feels so big. Is it very big?"

I couldn't say, "You're grotesque." I looked at her.

"You're like a clown. You've got an amusing nose and a black eye. Honestly that's all, and it'll probably be down by tomorrow."

Tomorrow, where will we be tomorrow? I wondered. "We must go on. Come on, I'll give you a leg up. Jennifer, wake up."

"I expect I'm suffering from a sugar deficiency, that makes people faint," she said, picking up her reins . . . "Are people shouting?"

For a moment I thought, she's going mad, then I looked behind us and in the distance there were ponies and people waving.

"You're right!" I cried. We stood and stared. "Let's hope they've got provisions. There's quite a few of them," I said, before I started to think about Desmond, and to hope he was still whole and not lying somewhere in the heather.

"I hope John's there," Jennifer said.

We waved. "Why don't they ride a bit faster?" I asked.

"Are there four or five?" inquired Jennifer.

We shouted "Hallo" and now we could see that there were three ponies and several dogs.

Heather and Raspberry whinnied. Then Miracle came bounding across the heather and threw herself against me, and I knew that Desmond was in the party. She licked my face, ran round me in circles, threw herself at my feet.

We started to walk towards the riders, calling "Hallo, this is super. Where did you disappear to?" We felt like cheering.

They came nearer and I saw that two people walked, one on each side of my dear dun Sandpiper and that her shoulder was covered with blood. I thought, she's shot, and imagined the vet, Mr. Macdonald, saying, "She will be no good, I'm thinking." And that would mean the knacker's cart.

And then I saw that she was sound and that the blood was coming from the Rumanian on her back.

"What's happened?" I called. "They *were* shooting at us then."

It seemed fantastic, like something out of a book.

"That's how we lost you. We meant to wait. It's Ioan. He's shot through the shoulder. I think he could do with a blood transfusion. Are we anywhere near a town yet?" asked Desmond.

We could see now that they were weary and blood-stained. We no longer felt like cheering.

"He fell off," Leslie said.

"Och, it was terrible," Roddy agreed.

I saw now that Ioan's shoulder was bandaged with most of my brother's favourite shirt torn into strips; Desmond was wearing his jersey.

"Luckily Leslie's done a course in first-aid," my brother said. His hand was blood-stained. "It's just a graze. There were plenty of bullets flying. It would have been fun if Ioan hadn't got shot," he said.

Leslie was riding Skylark; Roddy led Misty. Vintila and Desmond supported Ioan.

"We've got some food and a wee drop of brandy," Roddy said.

"It was a good thing we spread out. I suppose they recognised Ioan and Vintila. They didn't shoot at Roddy and Leslie, though I expect they saw them pass," Desmond said.

Rascal and Cockade lay down in the heather, their tongues hanging out.

I looked for Ching Poo. "He's dead," said Desmond shortly, catching my eye.

"Not shot?"

"He fell down a precipice. His sight has been bad for some time. I don't think he saw it," Leslie said, looking away from us all.

"One can't fight a battle without casualties. We went to the cottage and the old lady was wonderful. She fed us and filled our saddle-bags with food and gave us all the brandy she had," Desmond told us.

"A kind old lady if ever there was one," Roddy added.

"You look grubby," Desmond said.

"So do you," I answered.

"We saw a plane. We waved to it and I think the pilot waved back. It looked like one of ours."

All this time the Rumanians had stayed silent. Vintila looked hollow-eyed, but fit and strong, game for another ten or twelve miles. Ioan was pale and wretched. He seemed to be watching us without really seeing us. He held the pommel of the saddle with one hand, his other arm was partly strapped to his side. Blood had soaked through the rough bandage. There was blood on his face too, and his hair was matted with blood and sea water. Looking at him renewed my sense of urgency.

"Have you got a spot of brandy for Jennifer?" I asked. "She passed out; that's why we stopped."

Roddy found the flask. "It's getting late," he said.

"Her nose looks a mess," my brother said.

"Ssh," I hushed him. "I'm trying to keep up her morale."

We started to move. "Here, have Raspberry," I told Leslie. "We've had a pony each. Now I'm going to walk."

"What happened to you?" asked Desmond.

"Nothing much. We fled like cowards when we heard the guns. They seemed to be shooting at us. I expected one of us to be hit every second."

"We fled too. One can't do much without weapons, and one can't skulk very well on ponies. I made Misty zig-zag, but Ioan and Vintila aren't much good on a horse, they just held on and prayed, I think," Desmond said. "Then Ioan fell off and I had a frightful time getting him on again, and all the time there seemed to be bullets flying. I want to get near civilisation. The Russians may be following us now for all we know. But they won't dare to shoot at us once we're near houses." Desmond searched the hills with his eyes.

"The landscape is flatter at any rate," I said. "We came to a fence some way back, and a river and wires. We can't be far from Fort Angus."

"There's going to be a mist or fog soon. What weather for August," sighed Desmond. "All the same, I'm glad we came, I'm glad we got lost, and met Ioan and Vintila—so long as we get Ioan to hospital soon."

We started to walk faster. I helped to support Ioan. He kept his eyes shut now, but when Sandpiper jogged or stumbled, he gritted his teeth together and groaned.

"You can see why we've made such slow progress," Desmond said.

"You looked like the remnants of a defeated army returning home when we saw you just now," I said.

"But we're not defeated. We're returning scarred, wounded but in triumph," cried my brother.

"Touch wood," muttered Leslie. "Supposing nobody believes our tale. We don't look very sane."

"We'd hardly be bringing home a wounded man for fun," retorted Desmond.

The brandy seemed to have excited Jennifer; probably we gave her too much. She chattered incessantly.

"There must be lots of kiosks by Fort Angus. Wouldn't it be funny if we met Ian and John in one?" she asked. "What are we going to do first? Will our names be in the paper? I'll walk, I'm all right now."

We wouldn't let her walk.

"It's so silly. I'm all right. The brandy was wonderful. My nose doesn't hurt any more. I'll walk."

"No please. You might faint again. Please," said Desmond.

"It's only the brandy. It'll wear off soon," Leslie said. "Do you know you've cut Raspberry's heel, Sheila?"

"The front one, you mean? She got a flint in her hoof, I expect that did it," I replied.

Leslie was miserable and cross. I guessed that most of her life she had had her own way in all the things which really matter. Now there was no car and chauffeur, and poor Ching Poo had died, and we walked on hour after hour and there was still no sign of Fort Angus.

Roddy seemed tireless. He reminded me of a tough Shetland pony, which doesn't need much food, but which can keep going when larger horses are stumbling with weariness and tactfully suggesting to their riders that it is time their heads were turned for home.

Desmond might change as night came, but now he was wound up and nothing short of a bullet would stop him walking on and on until eventually he reached Fort Angus. Or that's how he appeared to me.

Vintila had a lost look about him. He must have found it strange to be rescued and hidden by a band of children on ponies. If only he spoke English what a lot he could tell us, I thought.

"Where will we be going first when we reach Fort Angus?" Roddy asked.

"Are you sure we're going in the right direction?" I asked, and for an awful moment I saw us walking on through another night to another morning.

"Yes, according to Desmond's map we'll be there quite soon," Roddy said.

"Just five more miles," agreed Desmond.

I felt elated for a fleeting moment; then I saw Ioan's face and knew we should hurry. He was growing weaker; his bandage was wet with fresh blood. Five more miles, I thought, and we're moving at a snail's pace.

Desmond's eyes followed mine, and his forehead puckered. "We could split up, I suppose. But even so an ambulance couldn't cross these moors, and a plane couldn't land. I think it's better if we stick together, don't you, Sheila?"

I thought for a moment, and tried to see myself galloping ahead on one of the ponies. I would stop at a police station or a hospital, if and when I reached Fort Angus. Would I take the map or leave it behind?

"You might fall off and then we would never find you," Desmond said, reading my thoughts. "You would lie on the moors and there would be a search party, and years later we would find your bones."

"How can you be so horrible?" I cried.

"It's quite possible. I can believe anything is possible now. It's better to stick together," Desmond said. He had put his grazed hand inside his jersey. I saw now that the sole was coming off one of his shoes.

"Surely we must reach somewhere soon," I cried.

CHAPTER TWELVE

No one answered my cry. For a long time we walked in silence. I held Ioan's stirrup, and tried to forget my aching legs. I told myself that every step was nearer to Fort Angus. I scanned the horizon for chimneys and watched the sky for smoke.

The dogs were beginning to lag; the ponies snatched greedily at bracken and branches; their expressions were sour; several times they all stopped at once, as though staging a strike. In the end we had to pick switches to keep the ponies going and that made us feel guilty, because they deserved a rest. But there was nothing else we could do, because above all we had to get Ioan to hospital.

We passed more sheep and once we saw a hind and fawn staring at us with startled eyes. "Look, aren't they sweet?" cried Jennifer, who was still cheered by the brandy.

Vintila muttered something inaudible. My legs went on walking. Sandpiper stopped a moment later; Miracle lay down.

"Walk on, Sandpiper," yelled Desmond waving a switch.

Sandpiper bent his knees. "He's going to lie down!" I screamed.

Desmond hit him and there was a groan from Ioan as Sandpiper leapt forward. "You've started him bleeding again. How could you, Desmond?" I cried.

"I didn't mean to. What was I to do?"

"Perhaps he needs a new bandage," said Leslie.

We looked at Ioan, but in the end we did nothing, because none of us liked to peel off the rough bandage he already wore.

"It's more important to get him to hospital," said Desmond.

"What about a ride now, Sheila?" someone suggested.

"No, thank you." Walking had become automatic. I didn't want the struggle of mounting. I was content to put one foot in front of the other, on and on, until we reached Fort Angus.

Presently we stopped. "It can't be more than two or three miles to Fort Angus now," Desmond said.

"Supposing we've been walking in a circle?" I asked.

"We haven't been."

The ponies dropped their heads and started to graze. Ioan opened his eyes. He stared at the hills. "*Rusi?*" he muttered.

"*Nu nu, nu Rusi,*" replied Vintila.

Desmond handed round pieces of bannock and a goaty-tasting cheese. We fetched water from a burn and mixed it with brandy; and now another twilight was drifting over the hills.

"You know we left the tent behind?" I said.

"What, the one we borrowed? Sheila, how could you?" cried Desmond.

"Raspberry wouldn't stand still."

"She always stands still; it's one of her virtues," cried Leslie.

"Well, she wouldn't wait for us to take it down. Neither of them would."

"Don't let's quarrel over a mere tent. It's an excuse to go back. We can stick up a placard, *This is where two Rumanians landed and were later granted asylum in the year* something," Desmond said.

"If they are granted asylum," replied Leslie.

I mouthed the word "Cross" and Desmond nodded. We ate the last of the bannock, put our mugs back into our saddle-bags and moved on.

Gradually the sky darkened, and then, for the first time there was rain—a slow continuous drizzle.

It was the kind of drizzle which, with time, soaks through your clothes to your bare skin. I suppose we all wanted to say something about it. I wanted to cry,

"This is the last straw!" But I couldn't. Instead I found myself fighting back tears of pity for us all; we seemed to have faced enough without having rain.

"Aweel it is nothing," muttered Roddy, half to himself.

Vintila turned up the collar of his jersey. The Rumanians had no coats—just cloth trousers, jerseys, and canvas shoes. I looked at Vintila's face. It seemed a face which accepted life as it was; but only up to a point, I realised. Otherwise he wouldn't have swum to freedom. His eyes were brown; he had a firm mouth which was set now in a straight unrelenting line. He saw me looking at him and said something in Rumanian.

"I think he's offering to carry you. Do ride Heather now," Jennifer said.

The effect of the brandy was wearing off. Her nose seemed to have grown still larger, while the rest of her had shrunk, so that she looked all nose and bones.

I wondered what her parents would say when they saw her. "I've got used to walking," I said.

"We must see the town soon," exclaimed Desmond, whose optimism had never wavered.

"We wasted too much time at the cottage," said Leslie.

"We only stayed long enough to get food," Desmond replied.

"Och, it was lucky the Russians didn't catch up with us there," said Leslie.

"It was the wee dog dying which took the time," Roddy told me quietly. "He fell down into a gully. We had to go down after him, knowing the Russians might be on our tail. He must have been killed outright; but Leslie wanted him buried . . ."

I could imagine the scene; the tears running down Leslie's face; everyone looking over their shoulders expecting the Russians, the Rumanians unable to understand the delay.

The dogs were beginning to tire. Miracle started to go on three legs; at intervals we had to wait for Cockade; Rascal dawdled. It went on raining.

"Perhaps the town has been alerted," Desmond said.

"What about?"

"Us."

"They don't seem to be doing much about it," replied Leslie.

"Will I be seeing lights in the distance? One at any rate?" Roddy asked.

I imagined a shepherd, followed by his dog. We stared into the rain and the falling dusk.

"Perhaps it's a rescue party," suggested Jennifer, and there was so much hope in her voice that I felt sure she saw her parents approaching through the rain with blankets and Thermos flasks.

"It's only one light; not more than a lantern," my brother said.

"It could be the Russians," I suggested. "We could have walked in a circle and be back you know where."

"Oh, don't. Shut up. Do you want to drive us crazy, Sheila?" Desmond cried.

"Of course it's someone looking for us. I knew someone would come in the end," Jennifer said.

"Let's shout," suggested Desmond.

"No, it may be the Russians," I cried. "Why shouldn't they be waiting for us? It's such a dim light. If it was a rescue party there would be lots of lights. They would be calling 'Hallo there!' or something. It's the Russians hiding behind a boulder waiting for us."

"Why aren't the dogs nervous then?" Desmond asked.

"They're too tired," I replied.

We had stopped, I realised. We stood in the rain and we didn't know what to do. It was nearly dark. I felt too tired even for tears. Ioan's face was grey and haggard. The ponies started to graze. A curlew cried mournfully in the sky.

I had frightened the others.

"We don't want to walk into an ambush," Desmond said.

"The light doesn't move at all. It's very faint," Roddy said.

"Like a lantern with a cloth over it," someone suggested.

I suppose the others thought like I did—a ship's lantern. Jennifer's teeth started to chatter.

"I suggest I investigate. I've missed most of the excitement to date. I'll take a boulder and go," I said.

"No, you can't," Desmond replied.

"Why not?" There were plenty of boulders. I picked one up. "I'm uninjured. I'm going. Keep Miracle."

I wasn't afraid until I was alone skulking through the heather; then a thousand possibilities rushed to mind: I saw myself shot and dying in the heather. I saw myself held as hostage; I saw myself wafted away to Russia. I saw the Russians laughing at me; I felt a bullet whistle past my cheek. Desmond called, "Sheila, come back."

But I went on; and the heather seemed to grow wetter and wetter, and I stumbled over boulders, and suddenly I was quite alone, and my mouth felt dry, my throat parched, and my teeth chattered.

I heard something rustle, and I lay flat with my face pressed into the peaty earth; something was coming

towards me; I gripped my boulder and waited for a light to shine into my face, for a hand to shake my shoulder. Instead I heard, "Baa baa," and sat up to see a black face peering at me.

I stood up calling myself a fool, and walked on more boldly towards the light which flickered now and seemed fainter, more like a candle burning low than a ship's lantern.

Sheep ran away from me through the heather. I could hear a burn running, and once the sound of a ship's hooter. I seemed to be on a path, and then suddenly I saw a building and I started to run, and imagined help, someone being sent to Fort Angus for a doctor and the police, a stable for the ponies, food for us. I saw myself rushing back to the others calling, "All right. Come on! I've found help." I hope the owners of the house believe me, I thought. But it wasn't a house when I reached it. I stood and stared; and felt deflated as hope drained away. I pushed open the only door and saw that inside someone had banked up a peat fire in the simple fireplace. It looked like a shepherd's hut. There was bread on the table, and a kettle near the fire; there was a bed in one corner of the room and two chairs.

I looked at the flickering fire before I went out again into the wet night.

"It's all right. It's only a fire in a hut," I called, feeling my way back along the path.

I felt utterly crestfallen. I had wanted so much to return with good news.

"It's all right," I called again. "Come on." There was no reply; only the falling rain.

"All right! It's all right!" I called. Supposing I can't find them, I thought. Supposing I've lost them.

"All right. The Russians aren't there. It's a light from a fire," I called. I started to run. I stumbled over a boulder. I got up again. My teeth started to chatter.

"Desmond, Desmond, can you hear me?" I yelled.

I saw myself alone running in circles. I think I started to cry and then I heard the others calling.

"We're coming. Coming." I waited for them, sweat running down my face, weak with relief. Their voices seemed to come from a great distance.

I thought, we can't go on like this much longer. Ioan will fall off; and then we'll have to carry him or strap him to Sandpiper; then Jennifer will faint again. The dogs will pack up soon. Oh, I'm tired.

"No Russians then," said Desmond, suddenly beside me. "Did you think you were lost or something?"

"Not really."

I must have stayed standing, because Desmond said, "Look, we've got to go on. It can't be much farther now. Wasn't there anyone in the hut?"

"No one at all," I replied, and my voice seemed to come from a long way away, almost as though it wasn't my voice at all.

CHAPTER THIRTEEN

I FELL down and Vintila picked me up muttering something in Rumanian.

"He says you're a brave girl," translated Jennifer.

"I'll lead her," Leslie said. Someone pushed me on to Skylark, reins were shoved into my hands, my feet found stirrups.

I realised then how stiff I was; and my bones ached. Then in the distance we saw lights again.

"Another shepherd's hut?" suggested Desmond.

"Fort Angus," said Jennifer.

The lights were spread out like Chinese lanterns on a hillside.

"There can't be so many shepherds' huts in the whole of Scotland," Desmond said with hope in his voice.

"Perhaps it will be ships out at sea," Roddy suggested.

"Raspberry's lame," Leslie said.

"Well, you've got two ponies. It won't matter too much," Desmond replied.

"I was going to show her in September."

"That's a hundred years away. You can't think of that now."

"We don't seem to be getting any nearer the lights," I said. I felt better now; I pulled my stirrups up a hole and spoke to Skylark. We could see now that the whole hillside was studded with lights.

"It looks like Edinburgh!" Desmond cried.

"We can't have walked that far," I said.

I had lost my hair ribbon and my hair kept falling over my eyes.

"If only it was day," said Desmond.

"Are hospitals open all night?" I asked.

"Of course," replied Jennifer.

"Poor Raspberry. Och, it's bad," Leslie said, leading her limping pony.

"It's not a stone again?" I asked.

"No. Her tendon's swollen. It's a strain or a sprain. She'll be lame for weeks."

"We've reached a road. Here, someone, help me with Ioan," cried Desmond.

The Rumanian was slumped across Sandpiper's withers. We still had some brandy. We managed to force the bottle between his teeth and presently he sat up again, and stared at us all with eyes which held both surprise and misery in them. He looked very weak.

"We must hurry," Desmond said.

There were telegraph poles running along one side of the rough road.

"We *are* getting somewhere," I said.

"It's about time we did. I have a feeling Ioan will pass right out if we don't reach somewhere soon," Desmond replied.

"Does Fort Angus have a hospital?" I asked.

"Of course; Daddy sends patients there," Jennifer answered.

"Where is it?" asked Desmond.

"About in the middle."

We didn't seem any nearer the lights. But at least the road made progress easier.

"Perhaps a car will come past soon and give Ioan a lift to hospital," I suggested hopefully.

"Perhaps the Russians will make a final attack," said Leslie.

"And shoot us all," my brother said.

"And that will be a happy release," I replied weakly, and suddenly we were all laughing, on and on, too tired to stop. If anyone had met us they would have thought us lunatics, but no one travelled along that rough road besides ourselves, and we went on laughing, all of us except the Rumanians. What they thought I shall never know. I imagined us dead and our mad laughter haunting the road for ever. Tears streamed down our faces.

"We must stop; we'll be in Fort Angus," cried Leslie.

"What a hope!" said Jennifer, and we were sober at last, and the lights seemed no nearer, and our legs were tired again and the ponies dragged, and the dogs walked stiffly, trying to save their sore pads on the rough road. It seemed as though we had been like this for weeks instead of days. Leaving home belonged to another decade; our encounter with the Russians might have taken place days ago, instead of yesterday.

"Have you read *The Small Woman*? The trek in that over the mountains was much worse than this one," Jennifer said to no one in particular.

"At least we will have something to tell our grandchildren," Desmond said. "Come on, Sandpiper. I shall have to use the switch. Someone hold Ioan."

"If only a car would come," sighed Jennifer.

I dismounted and held Ioan. "Come on, Sandpiper, walk on," I said. She had on her mulish expression, which appears only when she has reached the end of her patience.

"Don't hit her hard. This journey is enough to turn the best-tempered pony in the world sour," I said.

"We can't waste time. Ioan will pass out in a moment," cried Desmond, hitting Sandpiper.

The others had gone on ahead. We called "Wait," and Desmond said, "Do you remember how we used to call that after Mummy when we were little? 'Wait. Mummy, wait.' "

"Just," I said.

"Well, it was you who called it mostly."

"I bet it wasn't."

"What happened?" Leslie asked.

"Sandpiper stuck again," Desmond said.

We continued walking in silence, Sandpiper and Skylark walking side by side, Vintila and Desmond supporting Ioan. It was very dark now. We couldn't see the road any more but we could feel it under our feet. Gradually the lights grew nearer until they became lights in houses, and lights twinkling on ships and boats far out to sea; and street lamps too, I suppose, and car lights and lights in shop windows, and with them came civilisation: the road improved; we passed a shut petrol station. The moors became tame with wire fences and litter bins hanging on posts; we heard the distant sound of a train.

I wished we could speak to Ioan in his own tongue. I wanted to cry, "Not far now. Soon you'll be safe," and then the magnitude of what we were doing impressed me for the first time. But it may be miles yet. The road probably twists; perhaps there's a steep hill, I thought, afraid to hope too much for fear of being disappointed.

"Would that be a house over there?"

We could see lights and the faint outline of a long drive.

We stopped. "It might be on the telephone," suggested Jennifer.

"Och, it's too far away," Leslie replied.

We moved forward again and we could smell grass rather than heather now, and hear in the distance the murmur of the sea.

"We've nearly made it," said Desmond.

"Don't count your chickens before they're hatched," I quoted, afraid to believe his words.

"Vintila keeps thanking us," said Jennifer.

"It's too soon," I answered.

"Cockade's got left behind. Wait a minute," said Desmond.

Roddy called his dog.

"We're wasting so much time," I complained.

"Perhaps we should have stopped at the house after all. We could have telephoned for an ambulance," said Jennifer.

"If it was on the telephone," replied Leslie.

"Come on. Keep right on to the end of the road, keep right on to the end . . ." said Leslie.

The lights were growing larger and brighter. I felt empty and light-headed. It seemed odd to think that soon everything might be over; that we had sought adventure and found it. Our poor little tent I thought, all alone by the sea.

"I think I can hear people calling," Desmond said.

"Where? I can't," I answered.

"It's probably Daddy. I knew he would come in the end," cried Jennifer.

"I think you've got noises in the head," I said.

"Well, you're wrong. Listen. Can't you hear? People are calling—and look, they've got lights."

"Let's stop," said Leslie. "Raspberry's so lame."

"I shan't be able to start again," I answered.

"It doesn't matter, because there *are* people coming," Desmond said.

My legs crumpled under me. We had stopped, but there was still the sound of hoofs. I thought I was imagining things.

"We're suffering from illusions," I said weakly.

"Och no, not this time."

Cockade was yapping, but no one tried to stop him. I was sitting on the road, right in the middle. "I don't want to be run over," I said.

"It doesn't matter, they're on horses . . ."

Sandpiper was blowing down my neck; Miracle put her head on my knees. I thought, it might be Communists on horses. Why should it be help?

I could hear the clip clop of hoofs and voices calling now.

"It's John!" cried Jennifer. "Oh, Fearless, good dog. Down."

"Where have you been?" called Ian, in the voice parents use when you're late for tea.

And we've been away for years, I thought, we've met Russians and saved two strange men, and now everything seemed fantastic, as though it couldn't possibly have happened, not to us at any rate. I thought, it's a dream, I'm waking up . . .

But the road was hard under me, and the rain was wet, and my clothes clung to my tired body.

"We thought we would never find you; everyone's been ringing up. And the Macdonalds are furious about Tom Thumb."

He seemed to have come from another world. For hours Tom Thumb hadn't mattered; nor our parents' anxiety. We had been fighting to save a man's life, or so it had seemed; and we had been fighting for our own survival. But now suddenly we were facing life as we had lived it for so long. Suddenly Tom Thumb's cracked heels mattered; he might be out of action for weeks, and dear tiresome Ching Poo was dead; and we had let everyone down. We had only telephoned once; we hadn't sent a single picture postcard. For hours and hours our parents and nannies and uncles and aunts had been anxious; no one would ever trust us again. Gloom made me slump more than I need have done. I wanted to pass out and miss any unpleasantness. None of us spoke.

"I can't tell you what it's been like. And I've had to shoulder most of the blame. Where did you get to? John and I got back all right. We borrowed these horses."

"They look all in to me," said another voice. "Don't nag, Ian. They haven't got enough horses to go round anyway."

"Enough horses?"

I realised that David, another man from the base, had come. He had a nice voice, much nicer than Ian's.

"Are you all right, Jenny? There's been an awful row at home. This is the last time we're ever to ride with the Delmores . . ."

I thought, life won't be worth living any more. We're to have no friends. I saw people pointing at us, saying, those are those wild Delmores who got lost for days last summer; they're crazy. Honestly, they can't even read a map.

But now Jennifer was speaking.

"We have a very badly wounded man," she said in a small, matter-of-fact voice. "He needs a blood transfusion. Can you get an ambulance?"

I pitched forward on to the road then and the next moment the man from the station was lifting me up, and I could hear Ian's voice through a haze going on and on, taking me back to that first day when he cast a gloom over us all.

"A wounded man! How extraordinary. Why didn't you get him to a hospital? He looks as though he might die. David, what shall we do?"

My mouth was full of grit and blood. We seemed to have travelled a long way since the first day.

"We'd better move, Ian," cried my brother. "There is no time to lose."

"Come on, everyone," cried my brother. "We're nearly there."

I didn't want to be carried, nor did I want to ride. Quite suddenly I belonged to a battered, triumphant party, who had come back from the wilds undefeated like people in a book. We started to walk, dragging our tired feet and from the lights in front of us a clock chimed twelve times, announcing the start of another day.

CHAPTER FOURTEEN

David, who was dark and like a film star, wanted me to have his pony. I shook my head. I couldn't put into words what I felt, but I think he understood. Each second the lights grew nearer and the road smoother. My legs stopped dragging, and suddenly I was walking again. Our ponies raised their heads and looked.

The lights had dwindled but there were still enough to welcome us as we reached a street and houses. There were trees along the street and the smell of the sea, and the glow of street lights, and no people at all.

Ian was still talking.

"We had a job to find any ponies we could borrow. We've been searching all day. They even sent a plane out, but visibility was almost nil. The pilot thought he saw a tent, but that was all. And only one tent; it could have been hikers . . . We walked miles before we reached a kiosk and telephoned for Leslie's trailer. Where's the Peke, by the way?"

"Dead," said someone.

He should have left it there, but he continued asking questions and presently Leslie was crying.

"Down a gorge you say. Poor little beggar. How were you sure he was dead?"

We didn't say, "Shut up, can't you?" because he was older than us, a grown-up. Desmond changed the subject. "Anyone know where the hospital is?" he asked.

"Yes," said David quietly, as though he had been directing us towards it for a long time.

"Will it be the General Hospital?" Roddy asked.

"That's right; there's everything there," answered David. "We'll get hold of the police from there."

We trusted David; he wasn't like Ian—he didn't boss us, and he hardly talked, and yet we knew that whatever he decided to do it would be the right thing. We came to cross-roads where the traffic lights were red.

"It's all right; there's nothing coming." David said.

He was leading his pony, which was a roan Highland pony suitable for carrying deer rather than riders.

"It's not much farther."

Along the street a policeman was testing door handles. We turned down another road. We could hear the sea now softly breaking against sand. For a long time we had ceased to notice the rain; but the streets were wet and there was the sound of trickling water, and of a water-butt overflowing. On our left we could see the dim, towering outline of a castle. Miracle walked at my heels. Vintila and Ian supported Ioan. David walked steadily watching us, ready, I think, to catch anyone who fell by the roadside.

"So you left the tent? But it wasn't yours," said Ian.

Leslie hadn't stopped crying. Somehow one didn't expect Leslie to cry. I wanted to say lots of things to her, but I couldn't concentrate; in the end I said what Mummy says when young animals die or are killed for the pot. "Well, he had a short life but a merry one," and "At least he died quickly." But Leslie didn't answer.

She continued crying and we came to a gate and a notice which told one to "Drive carefully," not to hoot, and to look out for ambulances.

The drive had a hospital atmosphere; we didn't hoot, and we walked carefully and looked out for ambulances. There were notices directing us *To the X-Ray Department, To the T.B. Clinic, To the Maternity Wing, To*

Out-patients, and then at last *To Casualty Ward.* Our ponies began to falter.

Our dogs moved closer to our sides. The word *Casualty* was lit up. I began to wonder then what was going to happen to us all; the ponies could hardly sleep in the Casualty Ward, nor could the dogs. Were we going to fetch our parents from their beds? Or were they waiting for us somewhere in Fort Angus? I wanted to ask a great many questions, but David had handed his pony's reins to Ian and was striding into the hospital.

"I can't remember what hospital is in Rumanian," said Jennifer. I could see her now because there was a light in the courtyard where we stood. She looked ghastly. Once she had a cute nose which turned up at the end; now it was blue and fat, like a pug-faced boxer's. And her hazel-green eyes were bloodshot, and her feet had come through her shoes. I turned to look at my brother and saw that he had put his injured hand inside his coat. There were holes in his socks. He leaned against Skylark, his wet clothes hanging on him like sacks. Roddy hadn't any shoes; he stood barefoot in the rain looking like a boy who has no home and no one to care for him at all.

Leslie looked haggard, her hair hanging about her face. She didn't seem to care about anything any more.

"We've got here," I said to no one in particular, before David came back followed by three nurses and two doctors in white coats. They brought with them the smell of antiseptic, the smell of safety and civilisation.

"I think they'd all better spend the night with you," said David. "I'll take care of the animals, and we'll let their parents know."

"But I'm not ill!" cried Desmond. "I'm all right. I want to see the police. It's urgent . . ."

"Your hand is urgent too," said David. "You need to be washed and fed; the police can wait till morning."

We argued, but one can't get round doctors and nurses and presently we found ourselves inside the hospital while outside our faithful hounds were led away and we could hear the gentle clip clop of hoofs growing faint along the drive.

We had to give our names and ages. Desmond was very angry.

"I don't want to stay here. I've got to see the police. All sorts of things have happened," he cried.

"Wait till you see yourself in a mirror," cried one of the younger nurses, who was English and pretty, with blonde hair and very blue eyes.

A young doctor who Jennifer insisted was the Junior House Surgeon dressed Desmond's hand and gave him two injections, one against tetanus, the other a penicillin one. Meanwhile the rest of us gave endless particulars—our dates of birth, our parents' names, any illnesses we might have had in the past, dozens of things which all seemed totally irrelevant. Ioan had been taken by stretcher to the men's ward. Vintila was unable to give any particulars. Everything was brightly lit, which made us appear even worse than we had in the courtyard. Our eyelids drooped over our tired eyes; there weren't enough chairs to go round in the office and we sat on the floor.

A nurse led Vintila away.

"*La revedere!*" Jennifer called after him. Watching him go was like saying good-bye to nearly all our adventure. I don't suppose there's a Rumanian-English dictionary in the whole town, I thought.

The nurse Jennifer called Sister put down her pen. "That's about it. You'll be wanting something to eat next," she said.

"Yes, please, Sister," Jennifer answered.

"And your nose will need looking at," she added.

We followed her along the passage. My legs felt unbearably stiff. I only wanted to sleep. There was a table in the middle of the girls' ward with a faint light over it. Two night nurses were making up beds. It seemed a funny way to end a holiday. I couldn't remember the day or the date. I felt wearier than I had ever felt before in my whole life. The ward clock told me that it was twenty-five minutes past one.

Other patients stirred, turned over and peered. The nurse talked in whispers. I had never been in a hospital before. After our recent experiences it was like entering a new world.

My bed was in the middle of the ward. Forgetting that David had her, I waited for Miracle to come.

"Sit down on a chair; I'll get a bowl and you can wash before you get into bed. We'll bring you a hot drink and something to eat," the English nurse said.

The bed looked very white, and when I took off some of my clothes I looked very dirty.

"You've had some adventures, haven't you, I should say?" said the nurse. "You'll have your names in the paper if I'm not surprised."

I hadn't thought of that. I imagined a few lines on an inside page. It was lovely to be washed, to climb into the clean bed in a clean pair of hospital pyjamas.

"Now don't fall asleep for a second: I'm getting you a hot drink," said the nurse.

I lay down. Across the ward I could hear Leslie getting into bed. Desmond and Roddy were in the boys' ward; Jennifer's bed was next to mine. I thought, this is really happening to us, it's true, and then sleep came heedless of the hot drink, dreamless, blotting out the

ward and the hospital noises. From a long way away I heard a voice saying, "And I was going to offer her a sleeping pill," and then I slept.

I wakened to the sound of breakfast. Rain lashed the ward windows. I felt out of place; I didn't belong to a ward of sick girls, but to a tent in a glen. At the end opposite the door patients who were well enough were eating breakfast at a table. There was the soft sound of Scottish voices; the chink of china and occasional laughter. The air smelt of antiseptic; I felt far removed from yesterday. I looked for my clothes but they had disappeared. I saw that Jennifer was sitting up in bed devouring an enormous breakfast.

"I'm going to the X-ray department. They think my nose is broken," she called.

"Any news of Ioan?" I asked.

"They say he had a comfortable night."

"Have they told anyone about him?"

"I've no idea. Doesn't my nose look terrible? I nearly fainted when I saw it in the looking-glass this morning."

Jennifer looked at home in hospital. She talked gaily to the nurses, and continued eating. I longed for a comb; my hair felt like a tangled mane. I wanted to be outside again. I thought, a Highland pony must feel like this when he's stabled in a town after running wild on the moors. I began to worry about Skylark and Sandpiper. I wondered where Miracle was and whether she was missing us.

"If only I had clothes or even a dressing-gown," I muttered.

A nurse brought me breakfast on a tray.

"Aweel, aweel, you look better today," she said.

"I want my clothes please," I cried.

"They will be coming," she said in a soothing voice nurses use with fractious patients, so that I felt a nuisance immediately.

It was the best breakfast I had ever eaten.

"Aweel, aweel, I thought you had washed," said the nurse, reappearing with a bowl, towel and flannel.

"My toothbrush is in my saddle-bag," I said. I saw now that there were people lurking by the ward door.

"Who are they?" I asked Jennifer pointing.

The nurse smiled demurely at a young man in tweeds as she went out. "Reporters. The police are here too.

The day staff couldn't make out what had happened when they came on this morning," she answered.

"You seem to know everything. Oh, how I want a comb. Can't you throw me one? I'd get up, but I look so silly in these wretched hospital pyjamas," I cried.

"I saw Sister before she went off. She knows Daddy of course," explained Jennifer. "Mummy and Daddy will be here soon. I don't see how anyone can be cross with us now."

I hoped she was right. But supposing the Rumanians turned out to be spies, or escaped convicts after all? No one would be particularly pleased then. And it was the sort of thing which had happened before to Desmond and myself. Everything suddenly seemed too good to be true.

"You missed the early morning cup of tea," said Jennifer.

I don't care, I thought. More than anything else on earth I wanted to get out of bed. Surely the nurses will come to make the beds in a minute, I thought. I still felt stiff, and one of my heels was blistered.

I considered meeting Mummy and Daddy. I imagined them saying, "You won't ride again the whole holidays," but I knew they weren't like that. More likely Daddy would say, "How could you lose the way? You had a map, hadn't you? You are duffers. Really . . ." And Mummy would add, "You don't know how we've suffered. We've seen you fall over a million precipices, drown, break your necks . . ."

"Hallo," said Desmond, appearing in a dressing-gown three sizes too large. "They said I could see you now. I want to dress. The police are waiting and the Press . . ."

"Well, why don't you dress?"

"I haven't any clothes. They were wet, you remember."

"You'd better listen to the eight o'clock news. It's coming on in a moment . . ." said a nurse.

"Why on earth?"

Leslie was sitting up now. We waved, before we heard: "Two Rumanians landed in Scotland yesterday seeking political asylum. They were found in an exhausted condition by a party of children on a camping holiday and were escorted to Fort Angus where they are now in hospital suffering from exposure and lack of food. Inquiries are being made . . ."

"And that's the end of it all," announced my brother.

"Well, it's something to be on the news. At least we know now that they *are* Rumanians," I said.

"Well, we always did."

"Thanks to Jennifer."

"I wish I had some clothes. I feel like climbing out of here. Why should we be in hospital?" cried Desmond. The wild look was back in his eyes, and I suddenly knew that he was incurable—all his life he would want adventure. It was evident that he had already forgotten the discomforts we had suffered. Our adventures had merely made him more impossible.

"I want Skylark. I want to ride," he cried. "Where's the Sister?"

It was then that men in suits, in country tweeds, even in kilts started to bear down on us.

"You're the Delmores, aren't you?" they cried.

Cameras clicked. "I'm from the *Scots Weekly*"—"I want your story for the *Daily Times*"—"Can you tell me . . .?"

The Sister came after them, followed by the Matron.

"Not in here. Och, there are other patients. When will you newspaper men be learning . . .?"

They were shooed out—but others appeared.

"I'm from television. Can I have an interview?" announced one.

"Smile please. Cheese," said a young man with spectacles.

Then we saw the police waiting outside. And behind them our parents.

"I want my clothes," wailed Desmond. "Where are my clothes?"

There was the click of a camera.

A nurse came bearing clean clothes which we recognised as our own. "Your parents have brought these. Get into your cubicle quick," she said.

Desmond vanished. I said, "Where's my pony? What about our dog?" But she didn't know anything.

She drew the curtains.

"How are the Rumanians?" I asked. But she didn't know that either.

I want to say good-bye to them, I thought. Perhaps we'll be able to help them get settled.

Jennifer had been taken to the X-ray department. Leslie was sleeping again, her face pale in the sunlight which had suddenly, miraculously, flooded the ward.

I broke the comb Mummy had brought in my hair. I pulled my blouse on back to front. But at last I was ready. I pulled back the cubicle curtains, which Jennifer's father considered noisy, and stepped out with my hair in a pony tail again, my face clean, wearing a skirt and checked blouse.

I was myself again now, but somehow different too. It seemed fantastic that early this morning I had been dragging tired legs along a street with a wounded Rumanian on my pony.

Mummy and Daddy waved. "Come and talk," they called. There was the click of cameras. I crossed the ward.

"How does it feel to be these children's father?" I heard a reporter ask.

"Leave me out of this please," Daddy replied.

"It all seems so impossible now. I can't believe it really did happen!" I cried.

CHAPTER FIFTEEN

We saw the police before we had our interview with the Press. Jennifer kept pinching herself. "I can't believe it's true," she said.

Each of us was asked to make a statement. It took a great deal of time. Desmond's was the longest. I thought he would never stop talking.

A young policeman wrote down what we said. When we had finished, our statements were read back to us and we signed them.

Our interview lasted over an hour.

"You've done guid work," the young policeman said.

"Aye, they deserve a medal," said the inspector.

"It was nothing, and we fled when the shooting started," I replied.

"Will the Rumanians be able to stay?" asked Desmond. "And why were they on a Russian ship?"

"They were stowaways I believe, but why I don't know. Whether they can stay will be for the Home

Office to decide. I'm sorry we've kept you so long," said the inspector.

We shook hands all round and the constable said that we were brave lads and lassies, and the inspector called us a credit to Scotland.

After that we faced the Press. I can't remember everything they asked. At first they fired questions at us like a barrage, then they came more slowly. They had tried to photograph the Rumanians but had failed. They wanted to see our ponies, our homes, our dogs. At last the Matron shooed them out of the hospital, helped by a man known as the Chief, who was imposing, with iron-grey hair.

"He's very famous," Jennifer said. "Daddy knows him a little. He's one of the best surgeons in the world."

"Now we must go see Ioan and Vintila. We can't go without saying good-bye," Desmond said.

We found them together in a private room, which normally had only one bed.

They were shaved and washed. Vintila was sitting up with a chess-board on his knees. He looked much younger; yesterday he had seemed nearly forty, now he looked quite young, not more than thirty at the outside. He embraced us all. Ioan was lying on his back. He looked exhausted, but he managed a smile and a small wave of his good arm.

We said "Good-bye" and "Good luck" and Jennifer translated them into Rumanian. We said, "Come and see us when you're better. Get well soon," and "Eat a lot."

Then Jennifer cried, "Here's the Day sister. We'd better scoot."

We waved good-bye and smiled, and were suddenly sad and sorry that we had to leave them without ever knowing what they were really like or why they had left their own country to journey in a Russian ship and then to seek asylum in Scotland.

"They look hospitalised," Desmond said.

"Sane and civilised," replied Leslie.

"Quite ordinary," Roddy said.

"They'll be all right now. But I shall see that Daddy keeps an eye on them. I've got to come back to have my nose looked at again. They're waiting for the swelling to go down," Jennifer said.

"Perhaps they'll let you choose a new nose. You know, like actresses do sometimes," Leslie suggested.

"Thank you. I liked my old nose," retorted Jennifer.

"Och, I can't remember what it was like. I only know your lump of a nose now," Roddy said with a laugh.

"Life's going to seem pretty dull now. Do you think we'll be allowed to go for another camping holiday next year?" cried my brother.

"No, thank you," said Leslie. "I'll be absent next time. Raspberry looks like an overworked hireling, and you know the rest . . ."

We knew she was thinking about poor Ching.

"Anyway, come on, let's hurry. Och, don't you want to see your ponies again?" she said.

I realised suddenly that there were still two weeks of the summer holidays left. There was a Pony Club rally to look forward to, and this time it wouldn't matter if Miss Simpson didn't ask us to lead, or if Jennifer cried, because no one could possibly call us feeble or irresponsible ever again.

"Poor John and Ian haven't had much publicity," said Jennifer. "It seems unfair."

"Life is unfair," replied Desmond.

Then suddenly we were outside in the courtyard where we had arrived in the early hours of the morning. Mummy and Daddy were waiting in our battered old car and in the front seat was Miracle, looking very important. Nurses called "Good-bye."

Leslie's chauffeur was waiting. Her nanny called: "Come along now, your parents will be home in half an hour—worried to death they've been," in her nannyish voice. She didn't look at the rest of us, and I guessed that we would always be "Those mad Delmores" to her.

Roddy said, "Good-bye, see you at the Rally." And suddenly we were all separate again, going our own ways.

"Where are the ponies?" I asked Mummy.

"Travelling home by box. We thought they deserved a rest."

"David's in charge," Daddy added.

We looked at Leslie, and she was poised and elegant again. Roddy climbed into his parents' van. Jennifer was already comfortably settled in her father's Hillman.

We called, "See you at the Rally!" and then we were driving away from the hospital, into the streets of Fort Angus which had eluded us for so long.

"Well, you seem to have had adventures. Stop licking me, Miracle," Daddy said.

Mummy kissed us both. "My darling children, we thought we were rid of you for ever. Never again do you go for a riding holiday," she said.

"But they accomplished something," answered Daddy.

"It's made up my mind for me. I'm going into the Army," Desmond said, and suddenly he sounded quite different, almost grown-up. "I thought I would never make an officer, and who wants to stay in the ranks all their life? Now I think I might get there."

"Not on map reading," I answered, but I knew what

he meant. He knew now that he was capable of leading people, even if he had never led a ride at a Pony Club Rally.

"What difference has it made to you, Sheila? This is interesting. Stop licking me, Miracle, for the tenth time," Daddy said.

I said: "I think it's taught me not to judge people. We despised Jennifer and really her nose was broken which is probably enough to make anyone keep crying. And then she knew Rumanian and saved the day."

"That was a tremendous surprise," agreed my brother.

"We thought Leslie was tough, but she was more scared than any of us when the Russians came," I went on. "We were certain Roddy knew the moor like the back of his hand, and yet he lost us on the second day."

"And we were really wrong about Ian too," interrupted Desmond. "He's not really such a bad chap."

"I prefer David," I replied.

"Have you fallen for him? He's like a film star, isn't he?" Mummy said.

"He's going a long way," Daddy added.

"Well, have you more friends now?" Mummy asked. "I seem to remember you saying once that you had no friends..."

"That was months ago. We are going to see everyone at the Rally. Do you think we can have a party in the Christmas holidays?" Desmond asked. "With a fruit cup, or cider or something. Not a children's party . . ."

"They've grown up, Nora," said Daddy. "In less than a week!"

We all began to laugh then, and suddenly there was

a cattle truck hooting behind and David calling, "We won't be long after you."

We could see Skylark and Sandpiper through the open slats and I thought, we'll have to give them a good rest before the Rally; they've earned it.

The sun was shining over the loch, and reflected in the still water were the hills and the fir trees and the road we had ridden along so disagreeably, for now we were nearly home.

"Well, did you enjoy yourselves?" Mummy asked. We both cried "Yes!" for already the trials and tribulations were fading from our minds. We could see the cottage now, the perimeter beyond. "I feel as though I've been away a hundred years," Desmond said.

"What I want to know is why you decided to transport the Rumanians by night. Surely it would have been easier by daylight?" Daddy said, turning into the little yard behind the cottage. "Why ride by night?"

"Because of the Russian fleet. We felt as though we were watched by a thousand eyes," answered Desmond.

We saw now that there were strangers waiting by the back door.

"More Press," said Daddy in a resigned voice.

They came towards us crying, "The Delmores? Smile, please..."

"There's no need to hide," Daddy said. "You've brought two men to safety. You must be proud."

We stepped out of the car. We could hear a plane coming in to land, a curlew calling, the gentle sound of the sea. Everything was the same, but because we had changed we saw it suddenly with new eyes. The yard was smaller than we remembered it; and the plane seemed to be making a tremendous noise, and the gigantic hangars looked more alien than ever among the quiet hills.

"I'm quite crazy, I haven't got a thing for lunch," cried Mummy.

"You're Sheila, aren't you? Can we have a snap of you with your pony? You're a very plucky girl," said an English reporter with a portable typewriter under his arm.

"I don't think we're going to get any lunch," said Daddy.

This is really the end of my story, but before I write *finis* across my untidy manuscript, I think you should know that Desmond has gone into the Army, and that we see a lot of David, whom we like more and more. Leslie doesn't seem so rich now and next year she's going to London to train as a model. Jennifer is still at school; John plans to be a doctor. Ian has married and lives outside London and rides a dressage horse on Wimbledon Common where there are no bogs. Roddy hasn't changed, but then he always did seem to belong to the hills. As for me, next year I hope to start learning to ride properly at the Ashmore School of Equitation.

One day last summer the Rumanians came to see us. They had borrowed a compatriot's car and appeared in grey suits with white handkerchiefs in their breast pockets.

Desmond was home on his first leave.

"Here come some tax inspectors," he said, starting to dash for the house.

"They look like the Foreign Office," replied Daddy, who was mowing the lawn.

But when they embraced us all and handed me an enormous box of chocolates, we recognised them as Vintila and Ioan. They had learned some English, and said with pride that they were working in London. We telephoned Jennifer and she rode over on her new horse, and David appeared with a book he wanted me to read, and we had a reunion which lasted till dark.

We haven't seen them since, but we exchange cards at Christmas.